# SPECTRUM WORLDS

## CYBERPUNK UPLOADS - BOOK ONE

### SETH RAIN

Published by Human Fiction

ISBN: 978-1-9162775-5-7

Editing: Jane Hammett

Cover Design: Books Covered

# YOUR FREE NOVELLA IS WAITING!

Visit **sethrain.com** to download your free digital copy of the prequel novella: *The Rogue Watcher* and sign up to Seth's Reading Group emails.

# A BRIEF NOTE

I use British English spelling throughout this series. Not only am I a Brit, but this story is set in a futuristic London (or as you will discover: Lundun), and so it seems only right to use British English spelling. I hope this does not detract from your enjoyment.

Seth.

I wander thro' each charter'd street,

    Near where the charter'd Thames does flow.

    And mark in every face I meet

    Marks of weakness, marks of woe.

In every cry of every Man,

    In every Infants cry of fear,

    In every voice: in every ban,

    The mind-forg'd manacles I hear

Taken from 'London', from *Songs of Innocence and of Experience* (1789) by William Blake

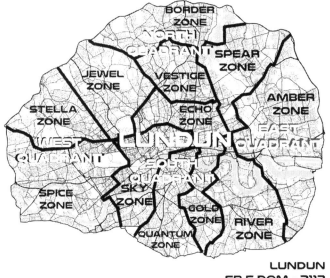

LUNDUN
FR.E.DOM · 2112

# SPECTRUM WORLDS

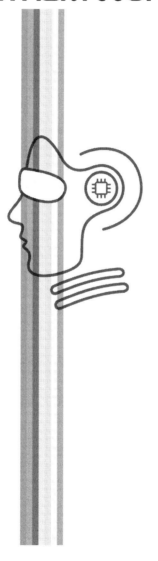

# PROLOGUE
## 2111

GRAFFITIED on the wall outside New Euston Station were the words 'God is android'.

The Postman didn't think God was android – or human, for that matter.

More graffiti further along the wall read 'God is love'.

Mia let go of his hand then hugged him, pushing her cheek into his chest. He kissed the top of her head. She gazed up at him and, on tiptoe, reached to kiss him.

'Don't wait,' she said. 'I don't like going into the station knowing you're out here waiting. It makes it harder.'

'I like watching you walk away.'

'Yeah – I know what you're looking at.' She raised an eyebrow.

'It's important that I see as much of you as I can before you leave me.'

She slapped his chest and tutted, then kissed him again. This time it was different, as though she was trying to tell him something.

They turned to the station, which was busy with early morning commuters.

'Six days,' she said. 'It's too long.'

When their eyes met again, he could tell she was about to cry. He stroked her cheek with a thumb. 'It'll soon go, then I'll be on this spot, waiting for you when your train comes in.'

She didn't look convinced.

'I love you,' he said, handing over her backpack.

She slung it over her shoulder. 'I love you too.' She smiled, but it came off as sad.

They held each other again.

She bowed her head. 'I have a bad feeling. Why do I have a bad feeling?'

'It's going to be fine. I'll have the bedroom decorated the way you want by the time you get back.'

She tried smiling again, then let go and backed away.

'Blue,' he said. 'Like you asked.'

She stopped and pointed at him. 'You promised – yellow.'

'I'm kidding.'

She waved, turned, and walked towards the main entrance.

Above the station, a Fr.e.dom drone-shuttle hovered before banking left and flying away. In Lundun, androids were never alone.

He didn't want to leave. She glanced back at him as she entered the station, her expression and body language hesitant, wary. He didn't understand why.

Then he saw the colours in his head, shifting from a deep red to orange, yellow then a dark violet. He saw himself standing outside the station, splintered, refracted. He saw different possibilities.

A choice.

Something was wrong.

It was happening more and more. It always hurt, made his head spin, but this was a different sort of pain. He closed his eyes and waited for it to stop, as he'd done so many times before. To stop it happening, he'd learned to choose one colour. But he didn't fully understand the choices he was faced with, and so chose through instinct. He'd tried to understand it, but those he'd told about it had put it down to a glitch, a misfiring inside his CPU. The world before him flashed yellow, then the colours vanished.

Mia had gone.

He told himself it was a glitch, nothing more.

To his left, a woman caught his attention. Dark-haired, dressed in a long black dress, black jacket, staring at him like she knew him. He had no idea who she was but, at the same time, she was familiar. It was unsettling, uncanny – as if he was reading her mind, and she his. Her expression communicated sadness or sympathy.

He turned back to the station. A flock of pigeons flew above New Euston's huge vaulted dome and vanished over the other side.

The dark-haired woman had gone.

A dull ache in his chest and nausea rolling in his stomach made him grimace.

Then the domed roof above the station lifted without a sound, as though something gigantic inside was trying to get out. Then the sound came. A massive explosion. The roof rose up and up, a yellow flower erupting from its middle. Then another explosion, and another.

He was thrown backward, landing hard on the pavement.

*Mia!*

More explosions ... relentless.

The drone-shuttle he'd seen only moments earlier had

broken in two and was spinning, falling. One part careened into the apartment tower to the east, sending a shower of flames and debris to the ground. The other part crashed into the station.

The world was ending.

But, without Mia, the Postman's world had already ended.

# ONE

## 2118

HE HAD ALWAYS BEEN the Postman. He was second-generation android. Of this, he was certain. As for anything else, he figured it was being hidden from him, a secret everyone else knew but him. But then, maybe every android felt this way.

The box wrapped in brown paper sitting on the bar in front of him was his last delivery before he retired. He didn't know what was inside it; he never knew what was inside the boxes.

'Are you the Postman?' a guy asked, taking the stool next to his.

The Postman looked him up and down. He was a big guy. Real big.

Lisa placed a Grit in front of the Postman. 'A double.'

Lisa had run his local, the Rose and Crown, for as long as he could remember. He took the Grit, glanced again at the man beside him, and took a long swig.

The big guy leered at Lisa. 'What about walking that sweet ass over here and bringing me one of those? Make it a large one. For a *large* android.' He winked his right eye, which started to glitch.

Lisa didn't say anything, just filled a glass and slid it across the bar.

The big guy licked his lips. 'You're a fine piece of work. Anyone ever told you that?'

'No,' Lisa said. 'I've run this place for ten years, seen all kinds of androids drink more than they can handle, and not one of them has looked at the one and only female in this place and said that.'

The big guy leaned sideways towards the Postman, his face all screwed up and confused. 'Is she joking?'

'I think she's being sarcastic.'

'And I think she needs to be taught some manners.'

The Postman hated the crap Lisa had to put up with. She never lost her cool, though.

'Hey,' the big guy said, turning his attention from Lisa. 'You the Postman or what?'

'Who's asking?'

'I was told I'd find him here. You him?'

The Postman swivelled round on his stool and tapped the postman badge on his uniform. 'Like I said, who's asking?'

The big guy's right eye socket leaked green alloy lubricant that ran down his cheek and onto his already damp shirt. He wiped his eye, then prodded it.

'You mind, buddy? That's kind of gross.'

With no warning, the android started to bash himself on the side of the head with a fist. He blinked over and over. 'Why haven't you chosen a name?'

'Don't need one.'

'Androids should have a name.' He pressed his dodgy eye back into his head. 'We need you to make a delivery.'

'I'm retired.'

The big guy frowned at the Postman as if he was a crackpot, and pointed to the box on the bar. 'Doesn't look like it to me.'

'It's my last one.' The Postman swivelled back round to face the bar. 'Then I'm kicking back.'

The big guy snarled, his upper lip curling. 'You'll want to take this job.'

'Is that right? What makes you say that?'

Rolling his shoulders, the big guy rocked his head from side to side, making a crunching sound. Then he scanned the bar as if to make sure no one could hear what he was about to say, and leaned in closer. 'We can get you out of Lundun.'

'Are you high?'

He smiled, real wide, his teeth black, his eye a tiny green waterfall of gunk. 'High?' he asked, looking confused. He was clearly one of the stupid ones, the sort built for a purpose – for bashing heads like the Postman's. 'I don't use Mirth.'

'Do you have the kind of Bits an android needs to get out of Lundun?'

The big guy was nodding like he'd only just learned how. 'Yeah. Sure. We can do that.'

'What makes you think I want out of Lundun?'

'Everyone wants out. We can help you.'

'I'm not interested in getting out of Lundun. All I want is to retire, drink Grit, and forget.'

'Forget what?'

'Everything.'

Again, the guy checked around the bar. As he swivelled back on his stool, his eye fell out, hit the floor and rolled away. 'Fuck!' He chased after it, barging past stools. Finally he reached it and picked it up. 'Goddamn eye!'

'I don't know who sent you, but I think you have the wrong postman.'

The guy examined his eye with his good one, spat on it, wiped it on his shirt, and put it in his pocket.

'Come on, buddy. Do you have to do that?'

'What's your problem? It's just an eye.'

'I know it's...' It was no good talking to guys like this. 'I'm retired, starting the minute I drop this off. If you need something delivered, talk to Zero.'

With his one eye, the big android stared at the Postman as if he was about to confess something he'd told no one else. The Postman leaned away as the big guy got closer; he smelled sour, like corrupt lubricant.

'This is between you and us. No Zero.'

The Postman didn't like the sound of that. If Zero found out he'd even talked to someone else about delivering, he was dead. It had taken a lot to convince Zero to let him retire – if Zero thought for a moment he was leaving to deliver for someone else, there'd be all sorts of trouble, the kind not even the Postman could talk his way out of. Being a member of the Brotherhood meant Zero was untouchable. The Postman had spent the past six years doing everything Zero had asked of him – to the letter.

The Postman got up to leave and picked up the box. 'Buddy, I can't talk to you about delivering.'

The big guy grabbed his arm. He was strong, his arm made of military-grade stuff. The Postman tried to pull his arm away, but it was no use.

'Who are you?' the Postman asked.

'What's important is who I work for – and what he can do for you.'

'Why d'you need me?'

There was no fighting this guy. Finally, he let go of the Postman's arm and sat down on a stool, then nodded at the one opposite, telling the Postman to sit.

'You all right?' Lisa asked the Postman, drying a glass and checking out the big guy at the same time.

Everything was wrong with the situation, and the bad feeling he had when he first saw the guy was only getting worse. 'All good. We're just having a chat.'

'We know you get shit delivered.'

'It's my job. When I deliver something, it stays delivered.' The Postman smiled, but his interlocutor didn't appear to have much of a sense of humour.

Resting a hand on the bar, the big guy lowered his voice. 'Some things are trickier to deliver than others.' His eyes narrowed meaningfully on the Postman, as if he was trying to convey something he should know already.

'I'm not sure I follow.'

The big guy stared at him then asked, 'What's in the box?'

The Postman shrugged. 'How should I know? I just deliver them.'

'Are you well paid?'

'What's that got to do with anything?' When he gave it some thought, the Postman hated doing what he did. He knew the parcels he delivered for Zero were dodgy. But then, so were the people he was delivering to. His conscience returned at times and he suffered bouts of guilt. But then he remembered, usually after drinking a lot of Grit, what had happened to Mia. Then he didn't care so much.

The guy leaned back on his stool and wiped his chin with the back of a massive hand. His empty eye socket wept like crazy, spilling green fluid every time he moved his head. It was gross but kind of mesmerising too.

'Don't you ever wonder what Zero gets you delivering?'

'It's best I don't know.'

'Don't you want to take a peek?'

'Hell, no. Like I said – it's best I don't know.' The Postman waited. He glanced at Lisa and shrugged. *What was it with this guy?* 'Do you even know who Zero is?'

The big guy shrugged.

'He's with the Brotherhood,' the Postman said. 'They run Lundun's underground.' He pointed at the floor. 'Literally. They're everywhere – beneath Lundun.'

The big guy's good eye blinked furiously. 'Go on. Look inside.'

'I don't want to look inside.'

'A quick peek.'

'I never look inside.'

'Look in the box.'

The Postman could see they weren't getting anywhere fast. He stood and grabbed the package, hoping this time the mountain-sized android wouldn't stop him.

'Hang on,' the big guy said, again grabbing his arm. He took the parcel from the Postman and placed it on the bar. The guy's mind was whirring – the Postman could see it. 'I'm going to open the box.' He took a pistol from his pocket and placed it on the bar. 'Yeah. I think I should open the box.'

This wasn't going to end well. 'Like I said. When I deliver shit, it stays delivered. I can't let you open it. Zero will know it has been opened before reaching the address. Which means I don't get to retire.'

The big guy smiled a stupid smile, his hand moving slowly, picking at the parcel tape. 'I'm opening the box.'

'You need to stop. I've never lost a parcel and I'm not starting today.'

The big guy placed one hand on his pistol.

'Buddy...'

The first piece of tape was free.

In one sudden movement, the Postman slid a pistol from his pocket, pressed it into the big guy's empty eye socket and fired. The guy's huge body jumped back off the stool and landed on the floor. The Postman stood over him and fired three more times into his massive head.

Calmly, Lisa tapped a few buttons on her digi-screen.

Positive the guy wasn't going to get back up, the Postman put away his pistol. 'Sorry about that,' he said to Lisa.

'No problem.' She placed another Grit on the bar. 'I've called Jo. He'll take him for parts. You'd better get out of here – Fr.e.dom soldiers will be on their way.'

The Postman looked up at the surveillance cameras.

'Don't worry,' Lisa said. 'They're corrupted. Can't have Fr.e.dom recording in a place like this, can we?'

'You're one hell of an android, Lisa. You know that?'

She turned away, blushing.

The Postman stared at the big guy on the floor. 'He said he could get me out of Lundun.'

Lisa faced him again, her eyes wide. 'The dream, huh?'

'Not mine.'

'What *is* in that box, anyway?'

He downed the Grit and stepped over the body. 'You know me.' He tapped the side of his nose. 'My middle name's discretion.'

'Yeah – I believe you.'

Truth was, he didn't have a clue what was inside the box – and he didn't want to know either. Knowing anything more than an address made his job a whole lot trickier. Someone once said that ignorance was bliss. He wasn't sure he'd experienced bliss for some time. But ignorance had certainly kept him safe.

# TWO

ALL ACROSS LUNDUN, pink flares lit up the night sky. It was midnight and the Zone borders were closing.

Maybe because he wanted this drop-off to go well so he could begin his retirement, or because of what had happened with the big guy in the bar, the Postman was on edge. Something about that android and what he'd talked about made him jumpy. It had made him think about Mia, and he couldn't stop going over what had happened in his head. He saw it time and again: the graffiti, the way Mia looked at him before turning away, the other dark-haired woman, the birds flying above the domed roof of the station, the explosion, the screaming…

He really didn't want to know what was inside the box, and now he wanted rid of it as soon as possible.

Lundun was dark and rainy. Lundun was *always* dark and rainy. West Quadrant had been on lockdown for two weeks for violating a curfew initiated due to a disturbance in Haven Square, Jewel Zone, three weeks earlier. But try telling the androids in WQ that – he wasn't going to. Fr.e.-dom's drones watched and recorded, but hardly ever intervened on the streets. Fr.e.dom worked in the shadows more often than not. Now and then androids went missing. No one knew why for sure, but many suspected it was for breaking curfews such as the one in WQ.

He no longer used lifts if he could help it – not since what had happened in Quantum Zone last summer. The damn thing fell thirty floors before the safety cable kicked in. He'd thought he was a goner. He'd heard how your life was supposed to pass before your eyes when something like that happened. Not for him. All he'd thought the whole way down was: *I'm going to die, I'm going to die, I'm going to die...*

The address on the parcel said floor eighty-one. No way he was climbing that many stairs, no matter how many lifts had tried to do him in.

The graffiti on the lift doors reminded him of the day of the Lundun bombings: 'God is Android'. The doors opened. On the back wall of the lift were the words 'God is Human'. WQ was all about contradictions. It was a conundrum. One minute you thought you'd made a friend; the next, your friend was selling you for parts. Best to keep to yourself in a place like WQ.

'Which floor?' the lift asked.

'Eighty-one.'

The doors closed and the lift shuddered into life before shooting upwards. He really hated these things.

'Floor eighty-one,' the lift said, the doors dinging open.

He stepped out with the box under his arm and scanned the doors for apartment three.

Standing outside a room were two women leaning against the wall, staring like they'd been waiting for him.

'Where are you off to, handsome?' one of them asked, looking him up and down.

'Apartment three.'

The woman next to her pointed along the corridor. 'Keep walking, good-looking. At the end.'

'What's in the box?' the first woman asked.

The Postman shrugged. 'I just deliver them.'

She winked. 'Postman, huh? You don't look the sort.'

They watched him closely as he walked past. He took his time, a hand close to his pistol. He thought about what the woman meant by that. What was a postman *supposed* to look like? When he was far enough away, he glanced over his shoulder. They'd lost interest and were talking to one another again.

Checking the doorways, he found number three and knocked on the door. He closed his eyes and told himself it was the last drop-off. Everything would be fine once this was done. Get this over with and he'd be ready for some downtime. He'd got a tidy collection of Bits he could spend on all kinds of well-earned trouble.

He knocked on the door a second time, then flexed his shoulders.

Someone on the other side slid back the lock and messed with the handle. The door swung open.

'Delivery,' the Postman said.

Framed in the doorway was a guy bigger than the one in the bar. The Postman swallowed and gulped, hoping the guy hadn't heard. The android examined the Postman as if he was lunch.

He took the box from under his arm and read the label again.

'Are you Stig?'

This seemed to annoy the guy even more.

'Postman!' a voice called from behind the giant. 'Come in, come in...'

The huge guy moved to one side. An android with a red

ponytail beckoned the Postman into the apartment. He checked the number on the door against the one on the parcel.

'Don't worry, you're in the right place, Postman. Come on in.'

He took a deep breath and walked inside, not liking it at all. Something was wrong with the whole drop-off.

'You're everything I thought you'd be,' red ponytail guy said.

The room was sparse and tidy. 'I am?'

The huge android shut the door and stood in front of it, arms folded, the muscles on his forearms flexing. A tattoo of a naked woman adorned each arm.

'The name's Stig,' red ponytail guy said. 'That's Trevor.'

'I just need recognition and I'll leave you with the parcel.'

'Please,' Stig said, 'have a drink with me. It must be thirsty work delivering all those parcels.'

'I've just had a drink. Thanks anyway.'

'Then have another.' Stig took two drinks from the table beside him and offered one to the Postman.

'Really ... I'm fine. Just need recognition.' He lifted the parcel for Stig to look at the barcode and take ownership.

Stig stared at the Postman with a wry smile, holding the glass out to him. The Postman saw he wasn't going anywhere until he'd shared a drink. *Why now? His last drop-off.* This sort of thing was always happening to him. He took the glass and drank.

'It's good, huh?'

The Postman nodded and drank some more. Sooner he finished it, the sooner he could leave.

'It's called cola. Enhanced with all the nutrients a well-built android like you needs.' Stig walked over to Trevor by the door and stared at him. Then he spun around quickly, clapped his hands, and pointed at the box.

'Do you know what's in it?'

*What was it with this box?*

'I just deliver them.'

'You're good at delivering, huh?'

'When I deliver a parcel—'

'It stays delivered,' Stig interrupted with a huge grin.

The Postman didn't like this one bit. 'Have we met?'

Stig shook his head. 'No. But I like to do my homework on the androids I go into business with.'

'Business?'

'I only choose the best. And from what I've been told, Postman, you're certainly that.'

'I don't know what you've heard, but I'm not looking for more work. In fact, I'm retiring as soon as I hand over this parcel.'

Stig's expression didn't change, like he hadn't heard a word the Postman had said.

'You work hard, huh, kid? You deserve a holiday. I bet you have Bits saved up for a good time, huh?'

'Something like that. But it's not a holiday. I'm retiring.'

Stig's expression became serious and he moved in closer. 'You go into business with me, and you'll have enough Bits to retire properly – in style. I can set you free.'

The Postman glanced at Trevor by the door, who was still staring at him as if he was a v-meat drumstick.

'This is the second time I've been propositioned today. Zero wouldn't take kindly to me working for someone else.'

Stig, for a moment, appeared to be losing patience. 'You made quick work of Bartholomew.'

'Who?'

'The android in the bar.' He tapped his own cheek, pointing. 'With the messed up eye.'

'How do you know about—'

'I think that's why Trevor over there is a little annoyed with you. They were good friends.'

Trevor wiped the side of his nose with a fist and snorted.

'He worked for you?' This, the Postman thought, was where the drop-off would start going south.

'I wanted to check you are who I've been told you are. I've heard wonderful things about the Postman. I just needed to see for myself.'

'I don't understand what's happening.'

'I wanted to make sure you got the parcel delivered. To see if you're as good as they say.'

'Well, here it is.' He tried to hand the box over again, but Stig wouldn't take it.

'Work for me,' Stig said. 'Zero was smart getting you to work for him. I need something very important delivered, and I know I can count on you.'

'Like I said, I'm retired. Zero and me – we have a deal.'

Stig shrugged, then took another delicate sip of his cola.

'Have you heard of Zero?' the Postman asked. 'He's with the Brotherhood. He wouldn't like you asking me to deliver for you.'

'Is that so?'

'I can have a word with him if you like. As long as he gets paid, I'm sure he'd be willing to deliver a package for you.' The Postman needed to get out of there.

'That's very kind. Thank you.'

'No problem.' He placed the box on the table. 'If I can have your recognition, I'll leave you to it.'

'And begin your holiday?'

'Retirement.'

Finally, Stig looked at the barcode and the vibration on the Postman's wrist told him the drop-off was complete.

'Thank you.' He sounded more relieved than he wanted to.

'Any time.'

The Postman turned to the door, but neither Trevor or the naked women on his forearms moved out of his way. He closed his eyes. This Stig guy wasn't done with him. In his head, the Postman visualised where his pistols were in his pockets, and worked out who to shoot first to give him the best chance of getting out of there in one piece.

'Does the service stretch to opening the parcel?' Stig asked.

'What?'

'The box,' Stig said, pointing at it. 'I want you to open it for me.'

The Postman raised his hands in the air. 'Hey, like I said, I'm retired.' He tried smiling, but Stig wasn't smiling back at him any longer.

Stig sat on a chair, crossed his legs and ran a hand through his ponytail. The room was silent. Finally, the Postman was forced to break the silence.

'You're not going to let me go until I open that box, are you?'

Stig shook his head. 'Like I say. I do my homework. I know what you want.'

'What I want?'

'You want to know why your woman did it.'

It took all the Postman's willpower to control his temper – he hated this crook talking about her, but he couldn't let Stig get to him. He didn't know how he knew about Mia. The Postman put on a smile, desperately wanting to shoot Stig in the head.

'You want to know why she killed herself along with all those people in the station.'

It took all his strength to stop himself reaching for his pistol. 'You don't know what you're talking about.'

'The surveillance cameras are pretty conclusive. Were you there? Outside the station – when it happened? When she did it.'

With clenched fists, his teeth grinding, he stared at Stig.

'That must have been something. Seeing that happen right there in front of you must have been … difficult.'

He couldn't speak.

'Do you believe what Fr.e.dom said? That it was a terrorist attack? But why would your woman help humans? An android blowing herself up for a human cause … it doesn't make any sense.'

None of it made sense. Which was why the Postman didn't believe it. He'd gone over what had happened again and again, until it had made him crazy.

'It was Fr.e.dom,' Stig continued. 'Think about it. They needed a reason to keep humans out of Lundun, to build the wall, and that was perfect.'

He wasn't getting drawn into this bullshit. It was exactly what Stig wanted. The air in the room was stifling; the Postman needed a drink. He needed to retire.

Stig pointed at the box. 'Open it.'

There was no getting out of this. At least the drop-off had been done. Zero wouldn't know he'd opened the box. He took a deep breath and walked over to it. He'd open it and then get out of there. Stig and Trevor watched. The Postman picked at the tape and pulled it across. A flap on one side lifted. He checked on Stig, but his eyes were on the box.

The Postman lifted the flap and looked inside.

'Fuck!' He jumped backward and reached for his pistols.

'Don't!' Stig said, unmoved, legs crossed. 'You won't last a second.'

The Postman glanced over his shoulder to see Trevor holding a pistol bigger than one of his arms.

Loosening his grip on his pistols, the Postman lowered them. 'Is that who I think it is?'

'Check again,' Stig said.

Leaning over the box, using the barrel of his pistol to lift the flap, the Postman peered inside. Looking back at him, one eye closed in a crooked wink, was Zero's head.

# THREE

'WHAT HAVE YOU DONE?'

Stig stood beside the Postman, peering inside the box. 'So now there's no conflict of interest. You can work for me.'

'Who are the hell are you?'

'Stig.'

'But ... who *are* you? How did you do this?'

'I thought the Postman didn't ask questions.'

'I rarely stick around to see what I'm delivering.' He pointed at the box. 'You know, because, well, it's never good news.'

Stig nodded. 'Very smart.' He pointed to a chair. 'Have a seat.'

The Postman half sat, half fell onto the chair. He wasn't too bothered about Stig killing Zero – truth was, Zero deserved it. But it made the Postman wonder what it meant for him. He didn't like himself too much either, but he didn't want his head ending up in a box.

'What do you want?'

'I've told you. I want you to work for me. You're going to help me make a lot of Bits.'

'What about the Brotherhood? They won't let you get away with this.'

'Don't worry. We can handle them.'

'Who's *we*? You keep saying "we". Who are you talking about?'

Stig opened another can of cola, poured it into his glass and drank deeply. 'That's quality stuff.'

'I can't just start working for you. The moment the Brotherhood find out I've delivered Zero's head, I'm a dead man.'

Stig raised a finger. 'If you agree to work for me, I'll protect you.'

'How can you do that?'

Stig clasped his hands together behind his head and rocked back on his chair. 'How many humans have you met?'

The Postman glanced at Trevor, hoping to see some recognition that it wasn't just him who thought this android had lost his mind. Trevor had lowered his huge pistol and was demolishing a v-meat chicken leg.

'Humans?' the Postman asked, grimacing at the sight and sound of Trevor eating. 'None.'

Stig faced the window looking out over the Lundun skyline. The Postman followed his line of sight and saw a dark, rainy sky above neon-lit towers that housed androids, many of whom he knew would be high on Mirth and hooked up to the Net. A drone-shuttle skimmed the top of the towers, its green lights blinking.

'There are no humans in Lundun,' the Postman said.

Stig smiled, his teeth shiny but for one gold one on the upper right. 'There are humans right here in Lundun.' Then he turned to Trevor, who had begun a second, even larger v-meat chicken leg. 'The Postman thinks there are no humans here in Lundun.'

Trevor smirked without taking his eyes off the food.

'Well,' Stig said, shrugging. 'There aren't as many as there were. It's tragic, really. Don't you think it's tragic?'

'I know what they did to our kind, so no ... I don't think it's tragic.'

'Got no sympathy for the species that made you?'

'They didn't make me. I'm second-generation.'

Stig stroked his ponytail. 'You're ruthless. I heard that about you. You get things delivered, no messing.' He clapped and then spoke loudly, almost shouting, 'The Postman gets goddamn shit delivered!'

'It was my job.'

'You never lost a package?' Stig asked excitedly. 'Not one?'

The Postman shrugged. 'Have to take pride in something.'

'Why do you hate humans so much?'

The question surprised him and he wasn't sure how to respond.

Stig scratched his chin and narrowed his eyes. 'Is it because of what you think they did to your woman? You think they made her do it?'

'I don't know what happened. I don't want to know. I just want to forget.'

Again, Stig's demeanour changed quickly. 'I need you to make a delivery for me.'

The urge to tell him he was retired came and went quickly.

'Will you do this for me?' Stig asked.

Something told the Postman this wasn't a request. 'What's the package?'

'It's ... unusual.'

Trevor licked his fingers, grinning.

'Unusual?'

'It's a human,' Stig said.

The Postman waited for Stig to tell him he was joking. But he didn't.

'It's a ...'

'Human,' Stig said. 'I need you to deliver a woman.'

'A *human* woman?'

'You're not much of a listener, huh, kid?'

'But there's no way I can—'

'I'm offering you all the Bits you can handle. A way out of Lundun, lose the Postman's tracker.' Stig nodded at his wrist. 'You can get out of Lundun and find out who offed your woman?' Stig shrugged. 'Or, do this job and you can kick back here in Lundun and drink yourself to death.'

'You're crazy.' The Postman stood and headed for the door but Trevor was in his way again.

'Postman,' Stig said. 'I need your help.'

'I don't have a choice, do I?'

'Everyone has a choice, kid. It's just that some choices can lead to unwanted repercussions. But it's still a choice.'

The Postman turned back into the room, again going over his chances of shooting his way out. Maybe it was best to go along with Stig and get out of the room. He could think of a way out of this later.

'You wait until you meet this human woman. She's beautiful. Drop-dead fucking gorgeous. You couldn't make one better-looking.'

This guy was serious.

'Do you like android women?' Stig asked.

'Yeah, I like women. Look, Stig, there's no way I can

deliver a human. If I get caught, we'll both be in big trouble. With Fr.e.dom and the Brotherhood.'

'If anyone can do it, you can. You're the Postman.' Stig slapped the Postman's back, then grabbed a coat from the chair, swept it across his shoulders and put it on.

'Wait. Where are you going?'

'Trevor and I have work to do. I'll send you the address.'

'I guess I don't get to retire...'

'You're too good to retire. For now.'

Trevor snorted again at The Postman, who fantasised about sticking his pistol in one of Trevor's eye sockets the way he'd done with the other big guy in the bar.

Stig waited in the doorway. 'Don't underestimate her. Watch her closely.'

The Postman nodded and watched them walk along the hallway towards the lift.

His wrist buzzed and displayed the information for the delivery:

Package: Lola

Locations: WQ213 to NQ112

*Lola? What kind of name was that? Goddamn humans...*

# FOUR

THE POSTMAN HAD little choice but to do the job. He needed time to work out what to do next. The pick-up wasn't too far away. He knew the place – a bar called Legs in Stella Zone, WQ. Not that he *knew* the place. It was mostly for first-genners and freaks who got off on androids looking and dressing like human women. It was messed-up. For so long androids were made to accept humans subjugating them, forcing them to do the menial work humans didn't want to do. But somehow, there were those androids who liked to watch humans dance. And more than dancing went on in a place like that. He didn't know what this human woman was doing there. Something didn't feel right.

Sitting in his apartment, he was meditating the way Mia had shown him all those years before. He needed to take a moment and focus. The colours in his head were happening more frequently, and the pain he was experiencing after-wards was beginning to trouble him. He'd stopped asking people about the colours – something told him it wasn't something he should advertise. If he could work out what was happening, then maybe he could learn to control it. But as it was, the colours appeared out of nowhere, disorientating him, and now causing him considerable pain.

Breathing deeply and slowly, with eyes closed, he saw again the single white light moving towards him. The light splintered into different colours that throbbed in a regular pattern. He let them cover him, never looking at them directly, but in his mind's eye, letting them move through him.

A dull roar from outside brought him out of his trance. It was the familiar sound and sensation of another space shuttle launching over in NQ. He gazed through the window but saw no sign of it. There were all kinds of rumours about what Fr.e.dom was trying to do with these space shuttles. But no one seemed to know for sure. Whatever it was, it wouldn't be good.

He collected his things and left his apartment.

The images of Mia entering New Euston Station came to him. This happened constantly and there was no escaping it. He'd seen the digi-screen recordings two days after the Lundun bombings. They'd been leaked. It was her, Mia, walking into the station. She was shouting incoherent stuff about how Lundun belonged to humans. Then there was a flash of light and the images stopped. It made no sense. He didn't understand how Mia could plan and do something like without him knowing something was desperately wrong.

He headed over to pick up his bike from Jonsey who was equipping it with the latest solar-charging batteries. The plan was to sell it for a load more Bits that he could then use to buy more Grit. The bike had been a part of him forever – from the moment he was issued the job as postman. The thought of selling it hurt a lot, but he wouldn't need to go very far once he was retired.

When he arrived at the garage in Stella Zone, WQ, immediately he recognised the increased power in his hover-bike. As they were testing it, the original pale blue light illuminating the rear solar-jet was now dark blue. He gave Jonsey recognition and straddled the bike. It bounced, hovering above the ground with the sensation of resistance that had always thrilled him. He patted the graphite sides between his thighs. From the very first time he got on one of these things, he'd fallen in love. Leaning over the bike, gripping the throttle, the solar-jet fired and propelled him quietly out of the garage. The familiar warm, spiced smell of the bike's solar-jet wafted over him. He was home.

No way he was hanging about in that part of Stella Zone without a quick getaway. Self-drivers and bikes were scarce that night, like there was a party happening that he hadn't been invited to. He wasn't complaining. It'd make the job a lot easier.

The delivery wasn't difficult in itself; there was no reason for anyone to think he had a human on the back of the bike. But he would have a monumental problem if anyone found out he did – a life-and-death kind of problem. There had been no humans in Lundun since Fr.e.dom expelled them following the human riots of 2082. The Postman didn't know this woman and had no idea what she was doing in Lundun.

This part of Stella Zone was a haven for every sexual fetish going. You name it, you'd find it there. The sexbots advertising it all were out in force from midnight. Not that they were needed these days. You could find anything you wanted on the Net for a fraction of the price. But there were still some androids who wanted the real thing. Whatever that meant.

Some androids had their sexual impulses subdued, even taken away completely. But others had had them enhanced. There was a big market for both depravity subduers and depravity enhancers. The Postman figured that which way you went said everything about who you were. Sometimes, he wondered why androids felt sexual desire at all. How did that even happen? Some said humans made androids in their image, in the most complete and basic way possible. He guessed there must be some truth in that. But that only made sense for first-genners. What about second-genners who were made by androids? Why did *they* have sexual desire?

The Postman hated humans for what they'd done, but there were still many androids who wanted to be like them – wanted to be a real boy ... a real girl. He didn't understand it, but what could *he* do? The only way androids would ever pass as human was if they took on all of humanity's characteristics. *All* of them.

It wasn't until humans were banished from Lundun that androids started to see themselves as equals. But the Postman knew they would never be equal. Humans existed before androids, who were made *by* humans. Androids could argue all they liked, for as long as they liked, but an android life was not comparable to a human life. It never had been. Not that the Postman would say that out loud in Lundun. But they all knew it. Deep down, they all felt it too.

'Hey, handsome,' one of the women outside Legs said. 'Good-looking guy like you don't need no bar like that to have a good time.' She lifted her dress to show a tangle of lace. She blew a kiss and her huge pink hair wobbled from side to side. 'If you find anyone half as good as me, sweetheart, you'll have one hell of a night. But good luck with that. I'll be here when you want me.'

The two bruisers on the door, enhanced with all manner of muscles, nodded as the Postman walked between them. The walls vibrated with a deep, throbbing bass line. Through the centre of the vast building ran a platform a metre off the ground, on which there were around twenty silver upright poles, around which androids pretended to dance like human women. On either side of the runway were rows of punters.

'What's a postman doing here?' one woman on stage shouted down to him. 'You got a package for me, big boy?' She pulled down her knickers and showed him her barcode, asking for recognition.

'Not today.'

'Asshole!' she said, snapping back her knicker string.

At the bar, he ordered two Grits and downed them. It had been a day and a half. He should have been enjoying his retirement. Instead of being at the bar like this one as a punter, he was still working as a postman.

'I'm looking for the boss,' he told the woman behind the bar.

'That right?'

He showed his postman badge.

She shrugged and then served another guy waiting for a drink.

'Give me a break. I've had a crap day. I just need to talk to the guy who runs this place.'

She sighed and rolled her eyes. 'His name's Georgio. Knock on the door at the back.' She pointed.

He gave her recognition for the drinks, transferring the Bits, then walked alongside the runway over to the door and was about to knock when a woman stopped him.

'Steady on, friend,' she said, raising a hand. 'Where are you off to?'

'Georgio. He in there?'

'Why?'

He showed her his postman badge. 'It's a pick-up.'

Her eyes narrowed on his lapel and badge. 'Wait here.' She went through the door.

Checking his wrist for messages, he was relieved to see no more jobs had come through. Just the open delivery of Lola.

The door opened.

'This way,' the woman said, standing to one side.

He walked through the door, his hands close to his pistols.

A short, sweaty guy emerged from a room to his right. 'It's about time!' He grabbed the Postman's arm and pulled him into the room. The guy walked backwards and forwards, mumbling to himself.

The woman who'd opened the door shrugged at him, as confused as the Postman.

'Stig sent you?' the man asked, rolling one hand inside the other. 'He said he'd send someone who can get this done. I still don't believe it.'

'Are you okay, buddy?'

'Okay? Am I okay? Of course I'm not fucking okay. I had no clue. I thought it was some kind of joke. But she looked so good, so I went with it. Saw Bit signs before my eyes. They said she came with ready-made lenses – no yellow at all.' He pointed to his own android eyes. 'This guy – he brings her in here and says I can use her on the runway. Said she'd bring in a fortune. I went with it because ... well ... you should see her!' He puffed out a breath. 'Her eyes,' he said, as if entering a trance, 'like two huge fucking emeralds. Like nothing you've ever seen before. Right there in the middle of her head. Natural. Real. No lenses.' He shook his head and walked over to the Postman. 'You need to get her out of here. Now! If anyone finds me with a human, I'm dead!'

'Where is she?'

'Sally,' he said to the woman on the other side of the room, jerking his head, telling her to go and get her.

Then he leaned in closer to the Postman. 'Have you seen one of them?'

He shook his head.

The trembling guy whispered, 'I had to check her over ... to make sure. She has no seams.' He covered his mouth then checked the room, took his hand away from his mouth and spoke again. 'No seams ... like ... anywhere. Not where you usually find them. Some of the androids out there on that runway would convince a handsy blind man they were human. But not if you know where to look. There's nothing on her. Nothing under her arms, beneath the hair, not even between her toes. She's ... she's fucking human.'

'I need your recognition, buddy.' The Postman held out his wrist.

Georgio nodded and blinked, making the Postman's wrist buzz.

'Watch her,' Georgio said. 'You can't trust them. She's ... she's beautiful.' As soon as Sally came back into the room, holding the woman's arm, Georgio disappeared through another door.

The human woman had long dark hair, green eyes. She was dressed in black trousers, boots, and jacket. He couldn't take his eyes off her.

'Fuck,' the Postman mumbled. How had Georgio not known she was human? He could see it from the other side of the room. It was difficult to explain how or why, but he knew.

Then it hit him. He knew her. He didn't know how. But somehow, he knew her.

'Are you the Postman?' she asked.

She knew him, too. He was in big trouble.

# FIVE

THE POSTMAN TOOK his bike around the back of the club. Georgio was outside, waiting with Lola, who was now dressed in a long black coat, a hood covering her head and face.

'She's all yours,' Georgio said, backing away then ducking back into the club before slamming the door.

It was just the Postman and Lola in the alleyway.

'How do you know who I am?' he asked her.

She lowered her hood, her breath forming a cloud. Androids breathed too, but he'd never seen human breath before; it was whiter somehow. At least, Lola's was.

'I hear things. I've heard of the Postman. That's you, right?'

He didn't want to answer her. 'We have to travel on the bike. Can I trust you?'

'What do you think I'm going to do? Jump off?'

'That's exactly what I think you might do.'

'You can tie my hands around your waist.'

She was playing games, trying to unsettle him.

'Just tell me you won't do anything stupid.'

She shook her head and pursed her lips. 'I promise. If you tell me where you're taking me.'

'North Quadrant.'

'Maybe a little more specific?'

'Vestige Zone.'

'Who's bought me?'

'I just make the deliveries.'

'So, you're going to hand me over to whoever paid the most?'

'I'm sure whoever paid has had to part with a lot of Bits. And they live in NQ. My guess is you'll be living in luxury. They're all first-genners out there – they revere humans. Especially humans who look like ... well, take my word for it, you're better off there than here walking that runway.'

She shifted her weight from one foot to the other and narrowed her eyes. 'So, you'll help me? If it's some weirdo, you'll take me out of there?'

'I'm just a postman. Who should be retired.'

'Lucky you.'

'I would be, if I wasn't doing this job.'

'I'm sorry that me being sold to the highest bidder has disrupted your plans.'

'Look, I'm sorry this is happening. But the truth is, if you hang about here much longer, talking to me, you're going to find yourself in deep trouble – the kind I won't be able to help you with. These androids in NQ have a lot of Bits; it's not like this place – not like WQ. You're going to be fine.'

'You would say that. The amount of Bits a person has says nothing about their morality or proclivity to evil.'

This was getting annoying. The Postman thought again about the plans he'd made that morning. His day had turned out a lot different to how he'd imagined.

'I'm pretty sure it does.'

'You really think so?'

'I know so.'

She raised her left eyebrow. 'You don't think much of humans, do you? I can tell.'

'No.'

'Why?'

He couldn't disguise a short cynical laugh. It wasn't for effect – he hadn't expected to laugh. 'All I ever hear about humans is how violent and cruel they are.'

'And you think androids are different?'

'I don't think much of androids either.'

'That's some way to live,' she said, and he felt childish for saying so. She smiled wryly. 'You're a strange one, Postman.'

He didn't say anything.

'So, do you think androids are better than humans?'

'Doesn't matter what I think.'

'I'm human and I think an android's life is worth the same as a human life.'

'You don't believe that.'

She lowered her eyes, staring intently. 'I do. Whole-heartedly.'

She looked like she meant it. Her eyes were intense, and again he was struck by the notion that he'd seen her before.

'Have we met?'

She shook her head. 'I think I'd remember.'

He told himself to stop staring into her green eyes. But he couldn't stop.

'Can we do this the easy way?' he asked, breaking from her stare. 'I'm making the delivery, whatever it takes.'

'Why don't you have a name?'

'What?'

'A name. Androids come up with their own names. Why don't you have one?'

'I never wanted one. I'm a postman. Simple as that.'

'But you won't be when you retire. What will people call you then?'

He thought for a moment. He hadn't given it much consideration.

'What are you going to do?' she asked. 'When you retire?

He was tired of explaining. 'Nothing. Other than drinking myself to death.'

She waited, clearly unsure whether he was being serious or not.

'You've given up?' she asked.

The pity in her eyes caught him off guard. Why was he talking about this with her – with a human? He didn't know what to say.

'I get it,' she said. 'Diving to the bottom of a bottle of Grit is far easier than learning to trust again. And you're only an android after all. What do you matter?'

'You know nothing about what it's like to be android.'

'Can I give you some advice?'

'I get the feeling I'm going to hear it anyway.'

Lola walked over to the bike and straddled the back seat. 'If you stopped feeling sorry for yourself, and thought about how you can help others, then maybe you might find you don't need that bottle of Grit.'

He stared at her, unsure how this human could talk the way she did. He got on the bike and felt her arms wrap around his waist.

'You sure you don't want to tie them?' she asked.

'Just hold tight.'

A blue flare rose and then arced across the sky. The quadrant tolls were open.

He went through the route in his head, wanting to take roads with no checks except border tolls. He needed a clear route from the club to the drop-off with no problems along the way. Deliveries always felt straightforward when he picked up the package. Everything was going to plan, but this was the most dangerous time. He told himself to concentrate, to plan with flexibility so he could make adjustments in real time if necessary.

Only certain people could travel between quadrants, a postman being one of them. Which meant having to stop and show recognition. If there was a way around that, he'd have taken it. But there wasn't.

'Don't say a word to anyone,' he shouted behind to Lola. 'And don't take off the helmet.'

She squeezed his waist to tell him she was listening.

The drizzle hanging in the air coated them and the bike as they rode through Jewel Zone up to the border into NQ and Echo Zone.

He slowed down to approach the toll. There were self-drivers and bikes in front and behind, and he kept checking his mirrors for signs that someone might be following.

It was his turn to pass through the toll. He gave recognition at the terminal. The digi-screen blinked green and the barrier rose. It was all going to plan, which was a relief ... and made him nervous at the same time. Tricky deliveries never went completely to plan – which was what made them tricky.

Speeding out of the tolls, he headed north for Vestige Zone. Already the air smelled cleaner, fresher, wealthier.

What Lola had said about delivering her to someone he didn't know bugged him. This kind of thing never bothered him; usually he didn't know what he was delivering, so didn't question it. But he knew this time; she was right behind him, her arms around his waist. He told himself again that, after what humans had done to androids, he shouldn't care.

He checked his wing mirrors and saw a bike he recognised from the other side of the tolls. It didn't feel right, so he slowed down to take a closer look. The other bike slowed down too. The Postman figured it was following them.

He knew it. It was never going to be a straightforward delivery.

Speeding up, he weaved in and out of self-drivers and bikes, all the time checking his mirrors. It was still there.

'What is it?' she shouted.

'We're being followed.'

She glanced behind.

'Don't turn round!' he shouted back. 'We don't want them to know we know.'

'I think the speed you're going will give that away. Are we going to be okay?'

He didn't answer. Leaning over the handlebars, he twisted the throttle. Up ahead, two bikes waited, one on either side of the road.

'This isn't good!' he shouted.

They passed between the bikes, which started after them, riding at speed. They were catching up. The road cleared ahead and the Postman figured they'd be able to outrun them.

Something pinged off the back of the bike.

'What was that?' Lola shouted.

'EMP sucker,' he said. 'Electromagnetic pulse. If one of them sticks, it'll sap the bike's power. They want us alive.'

He weaved from side to side, giving the pursuers a moving target.

Something was hovering above the bridge up ahead.

'Hold on tight!' Again, he gripped the throttle and sped beneath the bridge.

A drone. He'd rarely seen one up close. They had grown in size over the years, until now they were the size of small self-drivers. The two oval yellow lights at the front made them look insect-like. Now armed with all sorts of specialised equipment and firepower, androids stayed away from them whenever possible. The drone swooped behind the bike, its arms unfolding from its underside. It didn't have the Fr.e.dom decals – it was rogue.

'Get it off me!' Lola screamed.

He glanced back and saw the drone lifting Lola from the bike. The Postman swerved right, then left, but the drone followed, and finally had a tight enough grip to pull her off. It immediately stopped and turned back, with Lola hanging beneath.

The Postman skidded, took out a pistol, turned his bike around, and chased after the drone. As it was carrying Lola, her arms and legs flailing, it was slower, and he soon caught up with it. He shot once, twice, a third time. Smoke poured from the drone, shrouding everything so he couldn't see. He hit the brakes. The air cleared and he saw the drone come down on the other side of the bridge. He headed after it, all the time searching for the bikes that had been following them.

The drone was on fire, smoke showing the Postman the way.

He powered the bike off-road, skidding next to a jumble of metal and rising smoke. There was no sign of Lola. He jumped off, his pistols outstretched, ready to fire.

'Lola!'

Something moved beneath the bridge to his left. It was

Lola. She stepped towards him. He reached her and pulled her towards the bike.

'Stop,' a voice said. It must have been one of the guys on the bikes. A silhouette emerged, pistol raised.

The Postman raised one of his own pistols and aimed it at the dark figure. 'I wouldn't if I were you, buddy.'

# SIX

THE GUY HOLDING the pistol had long grey hair and beard.

'I really don't like pistols aimed at me,' the Postman told him. 'It makes me nervous.'

'Then shall we lower them?'

The Postman didn't want to take his eyes off him, but he was out in the open and needed to look around to make sure there was no one else lurking in the shadows. 'Go ahead.'

The guy lowered his pistol. The Postman did the same.

'Let go of me,' Lola said to the Postman, snatching away her arm. She straightened her coat, huffing at him like this was all his fault.

'Who are you?' the Postman asked the android with the pistol. 'What do you want with her?'

He appeared calm, not as though he'd just chased a postman on a bike. He pushed his pistol into a pocket.

'There were two other bikes,' the Postman said. 'Where are they?'

'It's just me.'

The Postman glanced at Lola, who was clearly as confused as he was.

'I need to take her with me,' the grey-haired guy said. 'She doesn't belong here.'

'That's not going to happen.'

'You're the Postman, aren't you?'

He ignored his question. 'We're leaving.'

The guy checked all around slowly. 'We need to talk.'

'Am I supposed to know who you are, buddy?'

'No. But I know who you are and I know things you should know. About Mia. About the attack that day.'

The Postman hesitated then raised his pistol again. 'What do you know about Mia? Who are you?'

'I know you see colours. The spectrum.'

The Postman wanted to say something but didn't know what. He stabbed his outstretched arm and pistol towards him.

'I can help you work out what's happening. You must be confused – unsure what the colours mean or are showing you.'

'Listen, buddy. I know what you're trying to do, but I'm delivering this package.' He took a moment to collect his thoughts. 'If you want to stop me, you're going to have to use that pistol. And I don't fancy your chances. What's it going to be?'

The guy raised his hands in the air. 'You need my help, Postman. I can show you the truth.'

'I don't need shit from you.'

The Postman walked over to the bike with Lola.

'You're a shadow,' the guy said.

The Postman stopped. It was the way he'd said it, as though it was supposed to mean something to him.

'I'm a what?' He turned.

The guy was gone. The Postman looked all around, but he'd vanished.

'Let's go,' he said to Lola. 'The crazy people are out in force tonight.' He wanted to laugh off what the guy had said, but he knew too much. Something was amiss with this drop-off.

'You did an impressive job of looking after me, Postman.'

'I told you to hold on tight. You let go.'

'That drone would have had you and the bike in the air if I hadn't let go.'

He got onto the bike and she climbed on behind him. He looked back towards where the guy had been, but there was no sign of him.

'You should have held on tighter.'

'Yeah,' she said, rolling her eyes, 'this was all my fault.'

'I should be done with all this.'

'That so?'

At first he thought she was being sarcastic, but there was a look on her face that told him she'd forgotten about his retirement.

He checked the address and directions on his wrist, then started the bike. 'The sooner I hand you over, the better. You're trouble, Lola. Has anyone ever told you that?'

She didn't say anything, but he could tell by the looseness of her arms around his waist that she was unhappy with him.

It took twenty minutes to reach Vestige Zone. He had visited this place, between Echo Zone and Border Zone, many times. It was where the Bits were – all of them.

The androids they passed stared at him and the bike with disdain. He hated this place. First-genners pretending they were human, spending all their Bits convincing themselves and others. It was all bullshit.

What the grey-haired guy had said about Mia had got to him. He had no idea how he'd have known anything about all that, but the way he spoke made the Postman feel like he knew something important. He'd always known that someone was keeping the truth from him.

He slowed down, searching for the address he'd been given.

'Is this the place?' Lola asked.

He thought she'd be scared. But she wasn't. He realised that he didn't know where the hell she'd come from. How did a human end up with someone like Georgio, dancing on a runway? *No – he shouldn't ask questions. Just deliver the package and leave.*

His wrist buzzed when he reached the end of the street. The place was smaller than the others: a glass box with a narrow wooden door.

He stopped the bike and got off.

Lola followed and stared at the glass box. 'Is that it?'

He checked the address on his tracker and glanced back along the street. 'This is it.'

Lola got off the bike, determination in her eye.

Before he had chance to knock on the door, a woman opened it. She was taller than the ceiling inside and had to bend forward. 'Are you the Postman?'

He nodded and showed Lola inside.

The tall woman was second-generation, made taller for some reason the Postman couldn't work out.

'We're taking the lift,' the tall woman said, showing them the way.

He patted his pockets to check his pistols were ready. The lift doors closed and they were moving down. He really did hate these things. The woman stared at the closed doors. The Postman glanced across at Lola, who now appeared scared, her eyes fixed on the tall woman's back and her tattoo: 'God is Android'.

Lola glanced at him, and for reasons he couldn't explain, he felt sorry for her. The lift stopped and the doors opened. The tall woman bent over and stepped out.

Lola didn't move.

Outside the lift he heard music and voices.

Lola edged closer and looked into his eyes. 'You can't stay. As soon as you can, get out of here.'

'What do you—'

'Go,' she snapped, and again he had the feeling that he knew her. 'Do you hear me? As soon as you can, leave.'

'Your buyer is waiting,' the tall woman said, bending down to make eye contact.

Lola looked at him again, as if she was trying to communicate something, but he couldn't understand what it was. She sighed, then exited the lift. He followed her.

# SEVEN

THE TALL WOMAN led the way, followed by Lola, followed by the Postman. The sounds of a party grew louder as they weaved through a narrow corridor and entered a huge domed hall. The music thumped through the cavernous building. Naked bodies were projected onto the expansive ceiling, humans dancing in time with the beat. Fluorescent lilac strobes flashed to the beat.

'This way,' the tall woman shouted over the music, leading them off in another direction.

The underground cavern went on forever, the ceiling held in the air with what appeared to be magic alone. They passed androids dressed like humans, their eyes tinted, their seams covered up. They didn't even look twice at Lola, presuming she was one of them.

A door opened into another corridor. When he closed the door, the dance music was muffled and he could hear his own footsteps and breathing again.

'What is this place?' he asked the woman.

She ignored him, her shoulders hunched, her head tilted to one side to avoid hitting the ceiling.

He glanced at Lola, who no longer appeared scared, only wary. They reached another door. It opened and they walked into a room where a guy sat in a black chair behind an enormous desk.

'The Postman,' the android said, standing. 'I was told you'd deliver, and here you are. A little late, but you made it.'

'We ran into a little trouble.' The Postman stood with his arms behind his back.

'I know you!' Lola said to the man. 'You came to the club. Who are you?'

'Yes, and I must apologise, Lola. I haven't been completely honest with you.'

'Who are you?' she asked again.

'My name's Rex.'

The Postman knew who he was. He worked for Fr.e.dom, and was one of the richest androids in Lundun. Other than Cardinal himself, the creator of Fr.e.dom, he was one of its most influential members.

'What do you want with me?' Lola asked.

Rex held up both hands. He was well built, state of the art, with barely any seams. 'I had to see for myself what I'd heard. Georgio didn't have a clue what he had on his hands with you. But I had to make sure for myself.'

He glanced at Lola, who stared angrily at Rex. The Postman could imagine what he'd done to her to make sure she was human.

'After my visit with you, I had to bring you here, Lola.'

The way his eyes moved over her body was creepy and the Postman fought the urge to take out his pistols.

'What do you want with her?' the Postman asked.

Rex eyed him up and down. 'I didn't think the Postman asked questions.'

It was the second time that day he'd heard someone say so.

'I need your recognition.' He offered his wrist.

Rex smiled weakly and blinked at the Postman's tracker, making it buzz. 'You're done. Package delivered.'

The Postman couldn't look at Lola.

'Please stay,' Rex said.

The Postman ignored him and finally turned back to Lola. He was expecting her to say something, but she simply stared ahead at Rex.

'My dear, all this is for you,' Rex said. 'All those androids out there are here to see you. To find such a beautiful specimen is far beyond our expectations.' Rex took his time, taking in Lola, biting his bottom lip. 'When I examined you, I was exhilarated, Lola. Now I am thrilled to share you with everyone here.' He moved closer and brushed her cheek with the back of his hand. 'But don't worry. I will only share you for a short while. You and I will be together for a long time. I'm going to take care of you. You are now my most prized possession.'

This guy was clearly insane. The Postman hated the thought of leaving Lola with him.

'Will you stay?' Rex asked him, smiling. 'For a short while, at least?'

He glanced at Lola, who shook her head, reminding him what she'd said about him leaving as soon as he could.

'Sure,' he said. He couldn't leave her there alone. Not yet.

Lola narrowed her eyes, reprimanding him.

He followed the tall woman out of the room and looked back at Lola one last time, but the door was closed. The tall woman showed him to the huge domed dance floor and bar, then left. The Postman ordered a Grit and offered to give recognition but the barman gave him a confused expression and told him the drinks were free.

'Give me two more,' the Postman said.

The entire place was alive with music, dancing and drinking. Those who walked past him saw his uniform and seams, clearly wondering what he was doing there. He wanted to tell them *he* was wondering what he was doing there. At the centre of the room was a round stage surrounded by a fountain. The fountain glowed with purple light, spouts of neon-lit water arching up and over. Above, drones shuffled about, delivering food and drink. The Postman watched the projection of famous humans on the ceiling. He'd never understood the fascination, but many of these androids were gazing up, their mouths open. He didn't get it. After everything humans had done ... still these androids looked up at them like they were gods.

He saw two women he had met in Stella Zone, WQ, years before. He'd always figured they'd make it to NQ. It was easy to tell those who were going to get there. You needed equal measures of arrogance and a love of everything human, and these two had both in heaps.

He drank more Grit. The two women asked if he wanted to go back to their place over in Echo Zone, NQ. They had Raspberry Mirth to get them deep into the Net, as well as all the Grit he could drink. Just as he was about to come up with an excuse, the music stopped, along with the spouts of water in the fountain.

'What's happening?' he asked the women.

'Rex has one.'

'Has one what?'

They looked at him and smiled.

'A human,' one of them said and laughed. 'We've never seen one. Not in the flesh.'

The music changed to slow building violins. The light on the stage changed to cream. Something was rising from beneath the floor of the stage. People whooped and gasped with surprise, then clapped.

It was Lola, with Rex. But they were so far away he could hardly make them out.

Then huge projections of the stage appeared on the walls. There were more gasps and applause.

'Oh my divinity,' one of the women said. 'She's stunning. So beautiful.'

Rex raised his hands in the air and walked in a slow circle, waving to the crowd.

Lola wore a long green dress, her shoulders bare, her dark hair loose. The images on the walls showed close-ups of her green eyes. There were shouts of approval.

The Postman couldn't take his eyes off Lola. She was both scared and beautiful.

*What was wrong with him?*

He imagined wading through the crowd, shooting Rex in the head, then taking Lola with him. His glass was empty and he thought maybe it was the Grit doing the thinking.

The revelry died down and Rex prepared to speak. There was a hush inside the dome. Rex circled Lola.

The Postman wanted to rip his head clean off.

'We are all here this evening,' Rex pronounced, 'to witness the rare beauty of the human female. There are few opportunities for us in Lundun to meet a human, but to see one who is so beautiful is a true privilege. An honour.'

There was another round of applause, this time more reserved.

The applause died down and Rex continued. 'Fr.e.dom has set us free. I have tried, during the time I have helped take the company forward in Lundun, to put you at the centre of everything we do. I want – and have always wanted – to make our time here on this planet the best it can be.' He paused. 'And if we all get rich in the process, then so be it.'

Laughter and applause filled the domed hall.

'I see humans as a reminder to all androids.' He edged closer to Lola, who stared straight ahead. 'Humanity had it all in the palm of its hand. And then lost it.' He touched her shoulder. 'She is beautiful. Elegant, remarkable.' He faced the crowd. 'My friends ... her kind will soon be no more. Let us honour them as our forebears, our makers, but let us not forget that it is us, androids, who will inherit the Earth.'

The shouting and cheering were louder than before.

Rex raised his hands above his head. 'You and I, my friends, will live and love and be happy. Gentlemen, ladies, I give you Lola!' He untied Lola's dress, and it fell to her feet. Lola was naked.

The crowd gasped, then applauded.

# EIGHT

REX WALKED about the stage with his arms raised, thousands cheering him. Lola straightened her shoulders and lifted her chin.

Rex waited for quiet before speaking. 'Humans are animals. They are different to you ... different to me. Humanity will die, but I for one admire their achievements.'

More cheering.

'There are those ignorant to what we know is the truth.' He pointed to Lola. 'This is where we came from. Everything androids are is the result of this species. Whatever the future holds for androids, let us never forget this.'

His audience were at fever-pitch.

Rex, towering over Lola, held the back of her head, leaned towards her and kissed her. Lola didn't move.

*What was this?* The Postman reached for his pistol, then stopped. No one else seemed to recognise how insane this was. He moved through the crowd, needing to get closer to Lola.

Rex pulled away from Lola, placed a hand on her breast and then let his hand trace her curves to her hip.

The Postman's hands itched to take out his pistols. He would easily hit Rex from where he was, but the security drones would kill him before he had the pistols out of his pockets.

He reached the fountain and moat between the dance floor and stage.

Lola spotted him. Her eyes opened wide. Again he remembered what she'd said about leaving as soon as possible. He wanted to tell her he was going to get her out of there, but he had no idea how.

Her lips moved – she was trying to tell him something. *Go.* She was mouthing the word. *Go.* He'd seen her before. It came to him again – her dark hair. Green eyes…

He shook his head. If he left her with Rex, there was no way he'd get her back. Who knew where he'd take her, or what he'd do?

Rex walked about the stage, enjoying the adoration.

Lola narrowed her eyes on the Postman, clearly annoyed. But then her expression softened, as if she wanted to tell him she understood, that she knew what he was thinking. But there was something else in her eyes – defiance. She mouthed the word *go* one more time – and it came to him. He remembered where he'd seen her before. It was the day of the Lundun bombings. She had been the woman outside New Euston Station staring at him, her expression sad and lost and filled with sympathy.

There was nothing he could do to help her. But he couldn't just leave. This was his fault; he'd brought her here.

Rex held Lola again and kissed her.

The Postman met Lola's eyes, but now there was something different in them. He couldn't read their meaning, but again his hands dropped to his sides for his pistols. She was going to do something stupid – he saw it. He could see it happen in front of him – the way she'd move, what she'd do. It all drifted before his eyes ... the colours again ... first crimson, then lime green. But there was no way out, no way to help her... His head throbbed, visions splintering ...

Lola grabbed Rex and spun him around into a headlock. It was impossible – there was no way a human had that kind of strength and speed. Then a pistol was released from a hidden compartment in her thigh. It jumped into her hand. She stabbed one of Rex's eyes with a finger and, like an android, appeared to be downloading. He'd seen it on rare occasions – androids taking data from another android's CPU – but it was rare. What was she downloading? Lola wasn't human ... she was android.

Androids pushed and screamed as they fell over one another.

Lola fired at security drones, grounding each with one shot, which again for a human was impossible. She pushed her pistol next to Rex's head and fired then let him go. His body fell to the ground. Two security drones opened fire on her. They hit their mark, but it didn't stop her. She knelt on Rex's chest and, without looking, shot him, then turned her pistol on the two drones. A second pistol sprang from a hidden compartment in her other thigh. She caught it and fired three more times into Rex's head.

More security drones swooped through the building towards the stage. She wouldn't last five more seconds.

Dropping a pistol to the ground, Lola punched a fist into Rex's chest, fractured with bullet holes, and unfolded his breast plate. She fired inside his chest, over and over, destroying his core. Then she stood, bullet holes peppering her chest, stomach and legs. She stood with her arms outstretched, her head lifted to the ceiling, her eyes closed, waiting, as though she was about to dive into water.

Again, time slowed down, but there was nothing the Postman could do. Bullet after bullet entered her body and head. She convulsed. He wanted to fire at the drones but knew if he did he was dead. Lola was thrown backward and landed on the stage, motionless.

None of this made sense. She wasn't human. But there was no way Rex wouldn't have seen that.

He wanted to go to Lola but it was no use. He'd never get her out of there. And with the damage caused, there was little chance of saving her CPU.

The security drones hovered above the stage then swept the crowd. He needed to get out of there. He headed for the exit. Everyone was doing the same, a free-for-all, androids screaming and pushing.

A message bellowed through the dome, telling them to remain where they were, that Fr.e.dom had been notified. He really needed to get out of there. Heading a different way to everyone else, he followed the corridors to Rex's office, hoping to find a back way out. He opened the door to Rex's office. Outside there were gunshots and more yelling and screaming. This wasn't good.

He searched Rex's desk for something that would show him a way out. Dropping to his hands and knees he looked beneath the desk. There it was: a switch. He pulled it and a mechanical shunting noise powered up behind him. The wall opened to reveal a lift. He got in and pressed the only button. The doors closed and the lift headed up.

He needed to think ... really needed to think. Lola was an android. But how had she fooled Rex? There was no way he'd have fallen for it.

The lift stopped. The doors opened onto a field behind the small glass building he'd seen on the street earlier. Sirens screamed. He needed his bike. He ran towards the street where he'd left it, and saw the street was already filling with Fr.e.dom soldiers and androids who had made it up from below ground.

He ran across the field in the opposite direction.

His wrist vibrated. A message from Stig: *You did good, kid.* Stig wanted to see him about another delivery. Something told the Postman he'd got himself into deeper trouble than he'd realised.

# NINE

WHATEVER HE'D GOT himself into, he was pretty sure his retirement plans were on hold.

Looking back, thinking about Lola, he'd recognised something wasn't right with her. It was after what happened by that bridge, with the drone. Something had been going on, but he couldn't work out what.

On the horizon, Lundun glowed its usual orange. Out there in NQ, you could see the stars. Looking down at the ground, he wondered how many androids were hidden away beneath his feet in NQ. He'd never liked this quadrant, and having seen what happened in that place had made him like it even less. He knew that some androids got off on the whole human thing, but he had no idea there were so many of them.

'Postman!' someone shouted.

He spun around, pistols ready. Out in the open, there was nowhere to hide.

'Hold your fire,' a black silhouette said.

'Who are you?'

'Angelus.'

'Who?'

The figure walked closer. It was the android from earlier – the guy who had wanted to take Lola. The Postman lowered his pistols. 'What are you doing here? How'd you get into NQ?'

The guy brushed a hand through his long grey hair. 'We have lots to talk about.'

'We do?'

'You saw what happened to Lola, didn't you?'

'What do you know about that? Were you there?'

He shook his head. 'No, I wasn't there.' He gazed up at the clear sky.

'Look, buddy, I need to get out of here. I'm out in the open and I'm still trying to work through what I've just seen, so you're going to have to excuse me while I run for my life.'

'Wait,' he said. 'I'm sure you can talk for a minute.'

The Postman was losing patience. He really didn't want to be sucked into whatever was going on with this guy. 'I'm out of here. There's a whole division of Fr.e.dom soldiers ready to ask a lot of questions. And I don't have any answers.' He walked away, ready to find a bike.

'You know something is wrong, don't you?'

The Postman paused.

Angelus spoke slowly, surely, as if he had rehearsed, 'Something doesn't add up, does it? And there's the colours you're seeing.'

Angelus had his back to him, again looking up at the sky.

'What do you know about the colours?'

Angelus took his time to scan the field. 'Are you familiar with the many worlds interpretation of quantum mechanics?'

'If we take Schrödinger's equations seriously,' the

Postman said, recalling pretty much all he knew about it, 'the result is the many worlds interpretation.'

'Precisely.'

'What has that got to do with the colours?'

Angelus inhaled deeply. 'Let us take it slowly.'

The Postman looked around nervously. 'Not too slowly.'

'The many worlds interpretation is a theory that has emerged from what we know about quantum mechanics. Imagine an electron. Before the wave function collapses, the electron could be anywhere and in any state. This is called a super position. The moment we interact with the electron, the wave collapses and probability disappears; the electron can be empirically identified to exist in one position. Let's take this further. An electron can spin either clockwise or anticlockwise. There are two states. If, as you say, we take Schrödinger's equations concerning quantum mechanics seriously, what this means is, when you measure which direction the electron is spinning, the universe divides in two. In one universe, you identify the electron spinning clockwise. In another, you identify the electron spinning anticlockwise. Such divisions happen constantly and in mind-boggling numbers. Normally, when these universes divide and branch into even more universes, there is no way of moving between them. We inhabit one of these, perhaps limitless, worlds.' Angelus was staring at the Postman, as if what he was saying was simply common sense.

'So, I'm seeing these different worlds?'

'Yes. You have the ability to read these many worlds and choose a path that is least harmful – or most advantageous – to you. Or one version of you, anyway.'

'This is crazy. I can't do that.'

'You can. The idea that there might be a computer or

android who could do this has been around for some time. You have this ability.'

'You're saying I can see the future?'

'It's not that simple. I'm guessing, and I want you to help *me* understand. But what I imagine, is that you can see the many worlds laid out in front of you, like a map or a maze. When you're under threat, you choose the path through the many worlds that is most beneficial.'

The Postman stared across the field towards Lundun, trying to take it all in. 'So,' he said, 'what you're saying is, when I make a decision, there are many other versions of me who make different decisions and could end up in a worse position than me?'

'Yes,' Angelus said. 'That's right.'

'Actual androids?' he asked. 'In *actual* other realities?'

Angelus nodded. 'As far as we have the language to describe the concept, yes.'

The Postman recalled moments from the past. He'd spent so long trying to understand what was happening to him. He'd seen the colours on the day of the bombing. He'd seen them too with the big guy in the bar, before Lola was killed. All the possibilities – or potential eventualities – had flashed before him.

'The theory suggests that you see a spectrum of decisions, like the spectrum of light.'

The Postman nodded. This guy was reading his mind.

'And I guess you feel out of control when it happens?'

The Postman could only stare.

'I can help you,' Angelus said. 'I *want* to help you.'

'You said you knew what happened to Mia. You called me a shadow – what did you mean?'

'Come with me. I'll explain everything.' He pointed into the darkness. 'I have a bike. Trust me.'

The Postman peered through the darkness but could see no sign of a bike. 'Why should I trust you?'

Angelus sighed. 'I can't think of a reason.' He walked away. 'Are you coming or not?'

Getting back to WQ would be difficult without a bike. Since Lola had killed Rex, Fr.e.dom would be on high alert. There would be drones everywhere.

The Postman followed Angelus. 'Hang on.' He got on the back of the bike and held on to the handle behind the seat.

Angelus started the bike and they were off, heading away from the centre of Lundun and towards the edge of NQ and Border Zone.

'Where are we going?' the Postman shouted.

Angelus ignored him. They flashed past the last quadrant markers north. The Postman's tracker buzzed. Angelus slowed down, then pulled over beside what looked like an old shack in the middle of nowhere. They climbed off the bike.

'Are you crazy?' the Postman asked, showing Angelus the tracker on his wrist. 'I'm still a registered postman. They'll think I'm trying to leave Lundun.'

Angelus held his arm, then his wrist, and examined the tracker. 'I'll see to it, don't worry.'

'Don't worry?'

Angelus opened the front door to the shack and invited the Postman inside.

'This way.' Angelus showed him to a lift.

The Postman hesitated, not wanting to be trapped underground a second time that night.

'Trust me,' Angelus said.

'You keep saying that.'

Finally, the Postman got into the lift and the doors closed. The lift began to descend. Angelus held the Postman's wrist, took a small gadget from his pocket and pushed one end into the space between the tracker and his arm. He'd always worn it. As far as he was aware, there was no way to remove it. Eventually, with one final push, the tracker stopped buzzing.

'Do you know what all this means?' Angelus asked. 'With Rex dead, it will throw Fr.e.dom into chaos.'

'No kidding,' the Postman said, scanning the lift for a way out in case he needed it.

'The government is sponsored by Fr.e.dom. The Bit system, the Net, the media, the authorities – all of it is under their influence.'

'So what happens now?'

'We keep going until we have stopped Fr.e.dom from controlling Lundun, then the other enclaves.'

'That won't stop because you've killed Rex. Others will be more than willing to take his place.'

'What Lola did was symbolic. She killed Lundun's head of Fr.e.dom, in his own home. We won't stop until we bring them down for good.'

'You can't stop them. They're too big.'

'We have plans.'

The lift stopped and the doors opened into a long, narrow room with terminals running along both walls. Androids sat at most of the terminals. The Postman recognised the sort: plug-in junkies, cyberjackers.

'What is this place?'

'This is Digital Skin.'

'Digital Skin? The terrorist group?'

'I've never liked that term ...'

This was insane. The Postman tried to take it all in. *Could things get any more fucked up?*

'Look – tell me what you know about Mia. Then let me go. I promise your secret's safe with me.'

Angelus slipped his hands into his pockets.

'Mia carried one of the bombs.' He stared at the Postman. 'I'm sorry.'

'It doesn't make sense. Why would she do that? I loved her. She loved me – she wouldn't have done that.'

'Those who did it were called Blood and Bone. A human terrorist group.'

'Who? How do you know that? No one knows who did it.'

'Fr.e.dom hid the facts. They want androids to hate humans, so it is better for them to let paranoia feed their fear. But they are only a small group of dissidents. We don't have to see all humans that way. Many of them are like Lola, who want humans and androids to live side by side.'

The Postman remembered Mia walking into the station. He recalled the images from the CCTV of her inside, shouting those words, before there's a flash and the feed goes dead. Sweating, rocking slightly, it was all he could do not to throw up. He'd seen what Mia had done. He was there. But listening to Angelus brought it all back again. None of it made any sense. Surely he would have known. How could he have been so oblivious?

'There's no way you could have known,' Angelus said.

'Of course I should have known. How could I have not seen it coming?'

'Other people are closed to each one of us. It is a harsh truth, but a truth nonetheless.'

'No,' the Postman said. 'I don't believe that.'

Angelus hesitated, then with a voice devoid of emotion, said, 'I'm sorry.'

The Postman saw now that he'd never got over what had

happened. He'd told himself he had. But this only confirmed what he knew deep down ... he'd never get over what Mia had done. A wave of anger came over him. What if it was true? How could Mia have done that to him?

'You look exhausted,' Angelus said. 'You need to rest.'

He wasn't sure he'd ever rest again. More than ever he wanted to lose himself in a bottle of Grit and drink himself into oblivion. Nothing mattered now. Nothing had mattered since that day he watched Mia walk away from him.

Then he saw a ghost.

It was Lola. It was really her, walking towards him. *How was it possible?*

'I'm sorry,' she said.

'Who are you?' He checked for bullet holes. But there were none. She was in one piece.

'It's me. Lola.'

Her green eyes shone back at him and he recalled what Georgio had said: 'two huge fucking emeralds'.

# TEN

LOLA WAS RIGHT THERE.

'I don't understand. I watched them shoot ... I watched it happen. They shot you. You were...'

Lola, dressed in all black, the way she had been earlier, edged closer. 'I'm sorry,' she said. 'I wanted to tell you everything, but I didn't want to jeopardise what had to be done.'

'I know you, don't I? We've seen each other before.'

She shook her head, but the Postman wasn't convinced.

'Back there, on stage, I watched them kill you.'

'I know. I'm sorry. You were supposed to leave. I told you. Remember?'

'I couldn't. I shouldn't have taken you there. I had no idea what they would do to you.'

'It wasn't your fault. You're just a postman, right? You just make the delivery.'

'But I...'

'You didn't have a choice,' she said. 'We want to change all that. We're taking Fr.e.dom down. Lundun is under their control and we're going to set it free.'

'This is all wrong. I thought you were human.'

'I am.'

'But ... I saw you download from Rex, I saw how strong you were, I saw the way you moved. A human can't move like that.'

'That wasn't me.' Her brow furrowed and she glanced off in another direction.

'I think I'm losing my mind.' He looked over at Angelus, who was listening to one of the hackers whispering in his ear.

'Do you remember what happened at the bridge?' she asked.

'The bridge? When the drone took you?'

She nodded. 'We made an exchange.'

'An exchange?'

'The person you saw on that stage was my shadow.'

The word triggered the memory of what Angelus had said to him.

'Angelus – he said I was a shadow. What does it mean?'

'I need you to relax and listen carefully. Don't lose it, okay?'

'You telling me not to lose it will definitely make me lose it.'

'When Rex came to see me at the club with Georgio, that was me. I'm human. But before you delivered me to Rex, my shadow took over.'

'What do you mean, *shadow*?'

'It's a kind of avatar. An android copy. My shadow was willing to make the sacrifice, knowing what it would mean for Lundun and the world.'

'Wait a minute. An android avatar? How is that possible?'

'It's possible,' Angelus said.

The Postman had so many questions and didn't know where to begin.

'You said I was a shadow. That I ... that would mean there's...'

'Let us explain,' Lola said. 'It's going to be okay.'

'Are you saying I'm one of these ... that I'm an avatar?'

'Maybe *I* should explain,' a familiar voice said.

The Postman refused to look, knowing who it was.

'This will all make sense,' Lola said. 'I promise.'

Slowly, swallowing hard, the Postman turned ... and saw himself.

# ELEVEN

THE POSTMAN THOUGHT of all the times he'd stared at himself in a mirror. He'd often found it unsettling. When he stared hard into the eyes of his reflection, he sometimes got the feeling the person looking back at him was a different person, a person in his own right. It had been fleeting at first, but then the sensation had grown until it unnerved him and he was forced to break his stare. Maybe this was the reason.

'Can someone explain to me what the hell is happening?'

The man who looked like him – no, who was identical to him – moved closer. The Postman backed away.

'The first thing I want you to know,' the man said, 'is that you are you. Whatever happens, whatever I tell you, remember that.'

'That doesn't really help.'

The man raised both hands, trying to calm him. 'I'm human. My name's Jack.'

'Yeah, I can see that, buddy.'

'You are ... you *were* my avatar. My android replica.'

'That's bullshit. What are you talking about?'

Jack smiled sympathetically then sighed. 'There were very few made. Myself and Lola were two of the humans used for the experiment.'

The Postman considered punching him in his face.

'Like I said, you're still you. But you're me, too. Your character, personality, decision-making – they're all related to mine.'

The room was spinning. The Postman had to make an effort to remain standing. 'This is insane! How are you doing this? It's a trick.'

Jack glanced at Angelus. 'I told you this was a terrible idea.'

Angelus stepped forward. 'Postman, we didn't want to do it like this. But we're ready and we're going to need your help.'

'My help?' His head was full of hot metal. 'But I'm second-generation. I know I am.'

'You're not,' Lola said. 'You were programmed to think that.'

'This doesn't make sense. None of it does.'

'We knew this time would come. You've been our eyes and ears.'

'You've been spying on me?'

Lola laid a hand on his arm. 'We could have taken you and done this against your will, without you knowing. But we don't want it to be that way. Work with us. Please. Like my shadow did.'

'I'm not killing myself for you.'

'No,' Lola said. 'Of course not.'

'What do you want from me?'

'We've taken the first step,' Lola said. 'Killing Rex shows we can get to them. The more people who see that Fr.e.dom are fallible, that they're not untouchable, the more chance we have of bringing them down for good. People will see we can do this.'

'What can *I* do?'

'We want you to go back in. We need you to continue being our eyes and ears. Make deliveries.'

'Is that where Stig came from? He's working for you?'

'For the right money, Stig will work for anyone.'

'Are you controlling me?'

'No,' Lola said quickly. 'It's not like that. Not really.'

'What do you mean, *not really*?'

'You are you,' she said. 'But it's complicated. They configured you *from* Jack. You and Jack think the same, you behave the same. The things Jack would do, you would also do. There was a time that Jack could make you do what he wanted. Now it's more like guiding. Like the way he guided you to Stig so you'd deliver my shadow. But his use of this ability has always been limited. For some reason, you and my shadow have always been more autonomous – androids in your own right. It began with your name. You should have been Jack. But you rejected the name from the outset. It was almost symbolic.'

The Postman had no recollection of this choice. He'd just always been the Postman. He thought back to the decisions he'd made over the last few hours. At no point had it felt like he wasn't the one deciding. But now he was thinking about who he actually was.

'No, you're lying. This is some kind of trick. Why are you doing this?'

'It's not a trick,' Angelus said.

'Are *you* one of them? Are you human?' the Postman demanded.

Angelus shook his head, his eyes sympathetic. 'I'm android. Like you.'

'A shadow?'

Angelus shook his head again.

'Why are you helping them? Humans hate us. They've done everything they can to kill every last one of our kind.'

'It's not that simple,' Angelus said. 'There are, and always have been, humans who want peace with androids. The enemy is not humanity; it is those who wish to control the planet. To control billions of lives, providing great wealth for the select few. I see the enemy as corporations like Fr.e.dom. It will be up to you to decide who *you* see is the enemy.'

'Help us,' Lola said, her green eyes wide and beautiful.

'I'm just an android. A postman.'

'You're more than a postman. You're more valuable to us than you know.'

The way she looked at him made him believe her for a moment. 'You'll contact me through Stig? You know he's a crook, don't you?'

'It's the only way,' Angelus said. 'It's for your benefit too. Go back to where you were in Lundun, as a postman, making deliveries.'

'Stig's crazier than you are. Does he know what you're doing?'

'No, and we want to keep it that way.'

'Now Zero's dead, there'll be all kinds of lowlife waiting to take me out. The Brotherhood aren't going to let what happened to Zero go unpunished.'

'Angelus will keep an eye on you.'

'He'll keep an eye on me? Well, that makes me feel all warm inside.'

'You'll be fine,' Jack said.

'Not you, buddy! I can't deal with you right now.'

Lola stood between them and touched Jack on his chest. In that one gesture, the Postman saw they were together ... a couple.

'I told them to do this,' she said, turning to face the Postman. 'I want you to be a part of the revolution. I lost a part of myself today, when my shadow died. She was prepared to sacrifice herself because *I* was prepared. But I know what it's like to be android.'

'How could you possibly know that?'

She was serious, her eyes staring into his. 'I know what it's like because it's the same as being human. I saw it in her. You deserve to know what's happening. You deserve to choose for yourself.'

She meant what she was saying – he saw it.

'We didn't *have* to tell you anything,' Angelus said. 'We could have continued without you knowing any of this.'

'So why *did* you tell me?'

'Because if we hadn't, it would make us no better than corporations like Fr.e.dom. They control people without them knowing. We don't want to do that. We want you to choose to help us.'

Jack bowed his head.

'And did you want this?' the Postman asked Jack.

'No. But I understand why Lola wants to do it this way.' He straightened his back and swallowed. 'Please, help us.' He then moved towards Lola and put an arm around her shoulder.

The Postman scanned the room and saw hackers tapping away at terminals. They didn't stand a chance against Fr.e.dom, or any of the other corporations around the world.

'What will happen to Lola? Back in that club? Is that it – she's dead?'

Lola nodded slowly. 'It took us months to make her convincing enough to get her onto that stage with Rex. There was no way she'd have been convincing as a human when examined closely, which is why I had to do it.'

'Why did she have to take your place?'

'You saw what she did. There's no way I could have done that. And she downloaded what we needed from Rex.'

She was right. There was no way a human could have done what her shadow had done to Rex.

'Don't believe everything you hear about humans,' she said. 'It's in Fr.e.dom's interest for androids to hate humans and for humans to hate androids. We want to help your kind throw off the shackles Fr.e.dom has put you in.'

'What do you know about Blood and Bone?' the Postman asked Lola.

She glanced up at Jack, then bowed her head. 'Not much. They were a human terrorist group.'

'I want to find them. If I help you, you have to help me.' Everything he'd felt since the day it happened collected into one emotion: revenge.

Lola appeared unsure, but nodded faintly. 'But it won't do any good. It won't bring her back.'

'Now I know who did it, who brainwashed her, I don't think I can rest until I've found them.'

'And then what will you do?'

'Kill them,' he said. His expression was cold, and he saw in her eyes that she knew he meant what he said.

'Will you help us?' she asked.

'Give me the chance to get even – and you have a deal.'

A smile of relief grew from the corner of Lola's mouth as

she moved past him. His heart thumped and his throat closed. Even now, after everything he'd been told about her, all he saw was Lola: her eyes, her beautiful face, her long dark hair.

What was wrong with him? He told himself how much he hated humans, and especially Jack.

# TWELVE

THE POSTMAN HAD LEARNED that those who longed for power were those who society really didn't want in power. A contradiction. The megalomaniacs were out there. Take a cartel such as the Brotherhood in Lundun. What society needed was someone in charge who could think rationally, sensibly, calmly. But what the Postman found with those in power within such organisations was that they had a deluded sense of their own importance and ability.

When the Postman had found the head of his previous employer, Zero, in a box, he knew there was already a war being waged in WQ over who would fill the power vacuum. This vacuum had to be filled – it was inevitable. Like a hole in the ground was filled with water and became a puddle, so too a hole in society was filled with control and became power. He knew who'd taken over Zero's outfit because the guy was right there, about ten centimetres from his face, staring back at him. Wan appeared to be upside down when, in truth, it was the Postman who was upside down, his ankles held by two of Wan's cronies. It was all about perspective. He could argue it was the rest of the world –

reality – that was upside down, and he was the right way up. But then, he wouldn't want to live the rest of his days in this position. No, some things weren't about perspective at all. There was no reasoning his way out of this one; he was the one who was upside down.

'So,' Wan said, his breath warm and fishy, 'I'm sure you understand when I tell you I don't want you delivering for anyone but me and the Brotherhood – including that heap of fuck-rust, Stig.'

Stig, the Postman's current employer, would not be amused. But the Postman had no choice in any of it.

'No problem,' he said to Wan. What else could he say? He was in no position to negotiate – which he was sure was Wan's intention.

Wan backed away a little. The Postman could breathe again without retching at the stink of his breath.

'This Stig,' Wan asked. 'Who is he exactly?'

'Look, Wan, I really want to help you out. Is there any chance these two can turn me the right way up?'

Wan glanced at his cronies, who let go of the Postman's ankles, dropping him.

'Thanks,' he said, rubbing the top of his head. He sat on the floor, gathering his thoughts and feeling kind of sorry for himself. He hadn't asked for any of this.

Wan sat at his desk and leaned back in his chair. He reminded the Postman of a bear – one of those huge brown bears, slow-moving, all hair and cranky. It wasn't as if he was *trying* to look like a cartel boss – maybe he'd always dressed that way. Some drug dealers were concerned with their image. Some, not so much. There was no correlation between how they dressed and success ... that he knew of.

Wan reached for a stack of small gold boxes on the table, took one from the top, and opened the lid. The Postman couldn't see what was inside. Wan took a tiny screwdriver, reached inside the box, and appeared to be turning a screw.

The Postman stood, brushed down his uniform, and walked over to Wan's desk.

'You know what this is?' Wan asked.

The Postman shrugged. 'Music box?'

Wan ignored his joke. 'Inside this box is the CPU of someone I've known a long time. A friend.'

Wan reached into the box again. The Postman peered inside to see the workings were clean, lubricated and shiny.

'Someone you knew?'

Wan used the screwdriver to point at him. 'You ever hear of Descartes' evil demon?'

'Was he a postman?' He knew who Wan was talking about, but he couldn't help making jokes when he was in trouble. For some reason, he thought it would make people such as Wan treat him more kindly. His theory had worked pretty well for long enough.

'Descartes was a philosopher,' Wan said, ignoring the Postman's joke. 'He came up with a thought experiment. He imagined an omnipotent demon whose desire was to deceive him – a thinking thing.' He wagged his screwdriver at the Postman. 'He wondered whether everything he experienced might be an illusion: sight, sound, hearing, emotions ... the whole shebang. He asked himself how he would know if that was the case, but couldn't come up with an answer. All he could say was that in some way, he must be a thinking thing. Quite clever, really. *I think, therefore I am*. Even if he was being deceived by an evil, malicious demon, he must exist as a thinking thing in order to be fooled. He could be a CPU in a box, and this demon could manipulate his experience of reality the way it wanted. There was no way to prove otherwise.'

The Postman's eyes rested on the box. He didn't like where this was going.

Wan tapped the box with his screwdriver. 'As I say, this CPU belonged to a friend. Or, at least, to someone I thought was a friend.'

The Postman heard himself swallow. 'You're the demon, aren't you?'

Wan's lips curled into a smile. 'I *am* the demon.' He put the end of the screwdriver inside the box. 'When I turn this screw, my friend experiences pain. More than pain. Maybe something closer to despair. It's difficult to understand what his experience is like, exactly. But his reality is not a good place. I think we can safely say that.'

The Postman nodded, staring at the box. This might have been the cruelest, most evil thing he'd ever seen. He felt spiders crawling all over his body.

'You'll work for me now Zero is out of the picture. The Brotherhood still needs you.'

The Postman couldn't take his eyes away from the stack of gold boxes. His mind raced with thoughts of what it might be like for those CPUs.

'Zero agreed that I could retire.'

Wan made a triangle with his hands in front of his face. 'Not for the time being. You're going to continue working. And I don't want you delivering for anyone but me. Are we clear? I'm going to be keeping you very busy and I need your single-minded dedication.'

He nodded. He had no choice.

'I have big plans for you. Are you my postman?'

The Postman glanced at Wan's two cronies. He really didn't want to end up in one of those boxes. *What was it with these crooks and boxes?* But Stig wasn't going to leave him alone either. His best bet was to hope one of them killed the other before he had to decide his next move. Or better yet, they'd kill one another.

'Sure,' he said. 'I'm your postman.'

'I'll send you the details of your first pick-up and delivery.' Wan got up from behind his desk, his bulk colliding with it, sending his pile of gold boxes tumbling.

The Postman faced the two metal-heads who had held him upside down. He took a moment to remember their faces. He wasn't done with them yet. He'd have his chance to get even – he always did.

The one on the left smirked at him. 'You have a problem, Postman?'

'I'm making a mental note,' he said.

The big guy narrowed his eyes. 'Of what?'

'Which of you two fuckwits I'm going to take apart first.'

The big guy went for his pistol and the Postman went for his. They aimed at each other's head.

'Hey!' Wan shouted. 'No killing in my new office. Not without my say-so.' He placed a hand on their pistols and pushed down. 'Get out of here, Postman. I'll be in touch.'

The Postman pushed his pistol into his pocket.

'And Postman,' Wan said, facing the window, his arms behind his back. 'Don't even think about double-crossing me. The slightest whiff of disloyalty and I will find you, and everyone you know, and use one of my boxes for each of you.'

With his eyes on fuckwit number one, the Postman opened the door and left.

# THIRTEEN

STIG WAS HAILING HIM. He answered.

'Postman! What's the story, kid?'

'Uneventful.'

'You don't sound too pleased to hear my voice. You ready to get back to work?'

He'd not heard anything from Angelus, or Lola – or Stig, for that matter – until now. Things had been slow for a week. Which suited him. He'd caught up with some Speed-ball games, as well as trying to forget about Lola by drinking too much Grit at the Rose and Crown.

'Guess I should,' he said.

Now he knew it was a group called Blood and Bone who had organised the Lundun bombings, he was going to find out what they'd done to Mia. He would find them and kill every last one of them. For now, he needed to bide his time.

'I want you over here,' Stig said. 'Collect and drop-off in East Quadrant.'

'On my way.'

'Straight away,' Stig growled.

'I'm coming.'

He got in the shower, still unable to stop thinking about Lola. Which made him pretty uncomfortable, considering she was with a human version of him. Or was he an android version of Jack? That was probably more accurate. Since he'd discovered he was a shadow, he'd been paranoid this other guy was in his head, and that when he thought about Lola, Jack would know.

What was the point in androids feeling this way about another person? It was not as if they could procreate. It was a throwback to their creation. Being made in humanity's image meant that androids had their desires, their flaws, and their appetites. Androids were human in all but name. They looked human, thought human, even acted human. But they were android. The Postman was android – first-generation – and worth less than a human. Androids dressed this up in all sorts of ways, but they were designed as tools, weapons, slaves, and would always be seen that way.

He changed into his postman uniform and headed outside. He reached the bottom step and found someone waiting for him.

'You really should call before you visit, Arch,' he said.

Archer was a writer for Fr.e.dom's media outlets. They controlled the truth in Lundun. Archer unpeeled himself from the wall he was leaning against and followed him.

'How are you?' Archer asked. He arranged the collar of his coat. No matter what was happening, Archer always in control. It had something to do with how slowly and precisely he moved, as though it was planned, considered.

'Feeling a whole lot better if you want the truth.'

'The truth? That's what my job's all about. I'm always searching for the truth. I usually get there. Eventually.'

'You write what they tell you to write – there's no truth in that.'

'There's no one else to write for. It's better that I'm on the inside for now.'

Archer was all right, but he had a bad habit of showing up when he wasn't wanted. Maybe that's what made a writer a good reporter – they sniffed out trouble.

'Are you looking for me?' the Postman asked, glancing behind as he strode away from his tower and into the wet Lundun evening.

'I wanted to ask you about something that happened a week ago.'

'A week? I have trouble remembering what happened an hour ago.'

'That's because of all the blows to the head.'

The Postman knocked the side of his head with a fist. 'Being a postman's a tough calling.'

'With everything that's happened,' Archer continued, 'it's been difficult to keep on top of everyday events.'

The street outside his apartment in Jewel Zone, WQ, was the main road that snaked through all four quadrants. It was pretty much the busiest road in all of Lundun. He liked living there – always had. Few people did, because of the noise. But he welcomed the noise – the constant hum of traffic and machinery. He couldn't imagine living anywhere else. Which made him think he had a pretty poor imagination.

'Did they find out who did it?' he asked Archer, knowing full well who it was. 'Who killed Rex?'

'We have a good idea.'

Archer gave him a funny look, like he thought he had something to do with it. It hurt that he might think that. It was true – but that wasn't the point.

'Who?' the Postman asked.

'A terrorist group called Digital Skin.'

'Is that right? I've heard of them. You have any leads?'

'I'm following a few.' Archer lifted an eyebrow, the way he did when he was suspicious.

'How can I help?'

At the crossing, they waited for cars and bikes to stop.

'There's a bar you go to: the Rose and Crown. Here, in Jewel Zone.'

'Yeah.'

'On the day Rex was killed, there was a shooting in the bar. I have a few witnesses and some inconclusive drone coverage. Nothing from the surveillance inside or outside the bar for some reason. You know anything about it?'

He took a moment to remember sticking his pistol in that big guy's eye socket. He shook his head. 'Can't say I do. I was in there that day. But I don't remember any shooting.'

'I guess it's something you'd remember.'

'I'd say so. What's that got to do with who killed Rex, anyway?'

'I didn't say it had.' He raised his eyebrow again and waited for the Postman to speak.

They crossed the street.

'You said you were investigating the murder.'

'I have a nose for a story,' Archer said. 'You know that. Something's telling me to follow this lead.' His tone changed, became more business-like.

'Am I missing something?' the Postman asked.

Archer took his arm and stared at him. 'I don't want you doing something stupid. We both know you're capable of it.'

The Postman nodded down at his own uniform. 'I'm just a postman. What do you think I'm up to?'

'You said you were finished with that. That you were retiring.'

'Change of plan.'

Archer released his arm. 'I have a bad feeling. And when you go missing, off the radar, it makes me nervous.'

'No need to worry. You just concentrate on finding whoever murdered that guy in the bar.'

People walked past them. Archer pretended to smile, to show nothing was amiss.

'I lost someone that day, too,' Archer said. 'Remember?'

Archer did this now and then – reminded him they were the same. Archer's partner, Jess, had both been killed in the Lundun bombings. That was how he and Archer had met. There had been all kinds of interviews and questions after it happened. He needed to give Archer something that would keep him off his back.

'I know who did it,' he said.

He saw in Archer's eyes that he immediately knew what he was talking about.

'How?' Archer frowned. 'How do you know? Tell me who.'

'They're called Blood and Bone.'

Archer's shoulders fell, and he blinked slowly.

'You've heard of them?' the Postman asked.

Archer exhaled noisily. 'Yeah. A human terrorist group. But I didn't think they had that capability. I hadn't given them much consideration.'

'They did it,' the Postman said. 'It was them.'

'How do you know?'

The look Archer gave him reminded him he was a writer for Fr.e.dom's media.

'I can't tell you. I'm not sure I should have said this much.'

'You'd tell me, wouldn't you?' Archer asked. 'If you'd got yourself into trouble, you'd tell me?'

'Of course. You'd be the first person I went to.'

Archer looked at him side-on. 'Now I can't tell if you're being serious. I'll investigate what you've told me. If there's anything in it, I'll let you know.'

The Postman slapped Archer on the back. 'You need to relax. Take some time off. You look like you need it.'

'We can't all be postmen,' Archer said.

'Guess not.' The Postman waved and headed to pick up his bike. He hated keeping things from Archer; he was a good man. But it was for his own good.

# FOURTEEN

WQ WAS BUSY THAT NIGHT. Sometimes, in WQ, there was a feeling, something in the air, that told you there would be trouble. Outside Stig's apartment block were three bikes with three Fr.e.dom soldiers standing around an android who lay stretched out on the street. The soldiers were looking at one another, as if waiting for someone to suggest the next move. The dead android they were staring at was a first-gen sex-bot, so no one took much notice. Some of the sex-bots had shaken off their old programming, but most of them kept doing it to maintain their purpose, appealing to some weird sense of destiny. They were designed to make men happy – human or android – and that's what brought them contentment. Without it, they were nothing. Sexbots were the first androids humans made. Of course they were. So most of them were primitive, which again suited humans.

The Postman pulled up his hood to avoid being seen and hopped up the steps into Stig's apartment tower. The lift, with its 'God is Android' graffiti, appeared to be working, so he pressed the button. The doors considered opening up. Reluctantly, they groaned and parted. He took a deep breath, stepped inside and told the lift the floor he wanted.

The doors opened at floor eighty-one. A conga of rats scurried along one wall, leading him to apartment three. He knocked on the door and Trevor, the android-shaped mountain, greeted him with a snarl.

'My postman!' Stig shouted excitedly from inside.

Trevor grunted at him as he passed.

'Are you rested?' Stig asked sarcastically.

'What's the package?'

'Straight down to business, huh, kid?' Stig licked his finger and thumb then pinched a trail of loose hair and pushed it into his ponytail. 'No problem. Our client was happy with your delivery of the human. It all worked out perfectly.'

The Postman wanted to tell Stig there was nothing perfect about what had happened to Lola, but he kept his mouth shut – the number-one rule for any postman.

'You did me a big favour, kid. I won't forget it. That lot who asked us to do the job have some deep pockets.'

The Postman nodded then glanced at Trevor who was doing a good job of both eating a sandwich and looking pissed off with him for shooting his buddy.

'You had any comeback from the Brotherhood?' Stig asked. 'Anyone been sniffing around?'

There was no way the Postman could tell him about Wan. Not yet. He didn't have the time or energy to deal with that. 'No – it's all quiet. Eerily quiet.'

Stig pursed his lips, taking a moment to check him out. 'Well, you let me know if there's any trouble.'

The Postman waited for the package.

Stig reached into the drawer of his table and took out a

small, rectangular parcel wrapped in brown paper. 'Here.' Stig threw it.

The Postman caught it. 'Send me the address.'

'On its way.'

He pushed the package into his bag and turned for the door.

'Postman,' Stig said.

He stopped.

'There will be more instructions at the drop-off. It's not your usual straightforward delivery. Don't let me down.'

He nodded, then waited for Trevor to finish his sandwich, open the door, and move out of the way.

In the hallway, he checked the address. It was a bookshop called The Book Worm in EQ, River Zone.

It was best to wait for the dead of night to make his way through River Zone. There were fewer people on the streets or the river and he could see the lunatics coming more easily. He checked his wrist for the drop-off address and headed under a bridge, down through Gattic Way and up towards the toll into SQ and then through to EQ.

He weaved his bike through traffic, flashing through the wet streets. The bookshop was just ahead. He left the bike and walked through the food market, avoiding stallholders' calls to try rice dishes, soup dishes or the newest low-grade Mirth extracts. The postman's uniform kept most of them at a distance, but some wouldn't take no for an answer. The important thing was not to make eye contact.

The bookshop was hidden down a cobbled street between a v-meat shop and a hair salon. It was dark inside. He checked his tracker. It should have been open. He pushed the door, which opened to the dinging of a small bell above his head. Inside, it smelled musty and tired. He walked to the back of the shop, between two tall shelves bursting with books. He had no idea what sort of android would be interested in these things, but there was clearly *some* money in it.

'Good evening,' a man said, appearing from behind the desk at the far end of the shop.

'Delivery,' the Postman said, looking around, taking the package from his bag.

'So it is.' The guy was short, had a round face upon which he wore large square glasses.

The Postman placed the package on the table. 'Need your recognition, buddy.' He tapped the barcode on the parcel.

The short man leaned over the parcel, lifted his glasses and blinked. The Postman's tracker buzzed. Another package delivered.

'I've been waiting for this one,' the man said.

The Postman scanned the shop, waiting for the instructions Stig had told him would follow the drop-off.

The guy unwrapped the package and took out an old red book. 'We really have to protect them.' With care, he turned the book in his hands. 'It's beautiful. Don't you think?'

The Postman shrugged. 'I don't read human books.'

'Don't you? That's a shame. This is a Charles Dickens. *A Tale of Two Cities*. Printed here in Lundun by Chapman and Hall in 1859.'

'Never heard of it.'

The guy didn't flinch. It wasn't surprising. Hardly anyone read human fiction. The Postman guessed that people who shopped in a place like this wanted a book or two to put in their apartment to make them appear sophisticated. History lovers.

The Postman straightened up. 'I don't mind some of their poetry. Human poetry.'

The guy raised his eyebrows and rubbed his chin like he was impressed. 'The name's Mole.'

The Postman nodded. 'Postman.'

'Haven't you chosen a name?'

He was tired of explaining, so didn't.

'Can I show you something?' Mole asked after waiting a short while.

The Postman glanced at his wrist, hoping to communicate to the guy to be quick. But already, Mole was heading down one of the corridors of bookshelves. The Postman followed and found Mole standing on a small stepladder, reaching for a book on a high shelf. Mole climbed down holding a small, tattered brown book as if it was about to explode, and offered it to the Postman.

'What is it?'

'Take a look. You say you like poetry. Have you heard of him? William Blake?'

The Postman placed his hands on the leathery cover of the book. 'I don't think so.'

'He was a remarkable poet,' Mole's eyes were on the book in the Postman's hands. 'And an engraver.'

Inside the book were colourful drawings. It wasn't what he was expecting at all. And the colours were familiar. Then it struck him – they were the colours he saw in the spectrum. The pale blues and natural greens. The reds of sunsets and fire. The writing was difficult to read at first, but then he began to follow some of the lines. He came to a poem called 'London'.

'It's the old spelling,' Mole said, moving beside him to read it. 'Blake had visions. He said he saw angels in the shards of light that cut through the branches of trees. He conversed with great people from history.'

'Visions?' the Postman asked. His eyes focused again on

the colours in the images. It was as though maybe this human, living over three hundred years ago, had experienced what he had seen. But that was impossible.

'His work was not read in his lifetime,' Mole said. 'It wasn't until years later that readers recognised his genius. He was a true radical – a revolutionist at heart.'

The Postman followed the lines of the poem, 'London', and was mesmerised.

Mole read aloud, 'I wander through each chartered street, near where the chartered Thames does flow. And mark in every face I meet, Marks of weakness, marks of woe.'

'That could be now,' the Postman said, glancing out of the window at the street.

'Human or android,' Mole said, 'the exploitation of the weak by those in power is an unavoidable truth.'

'It doesn't have to be that way.'

'Maybe not.' Mole read more of the poem. 'In every cry of every man, In every infant's cry of fear, In every voice: in every ban, The mind-forged manacles I hear.'

The Postman considered that last line. 'They're not real...'

Mole appeared confused.

The Postman spoke as if in a trance, '"The mind-forged manacles". They can be removed.'

'I don't see how.' Mole closed the book and handed it to the Postman. 'Take it.'

Staring at it, the Postman saw a truly priceless, beautiful object. He had few possessions, and didn't want to begin collecting them now. He shook his head. 'It wouldn't be safe with me.'

'It won't last forever,' Mole said. 'It needs to be read.' He thrust the book towards him again. 'Take it.'

Finally, the Postman accepted the book and pushed it into his postbag.

Mole walked through the bookshelves back to the desk at the rear of the shop. 'They'll be ready in a few hours.'

'What will?'

Mole rolled his eyes. 'The coding enhancers.'

'Look, buddy, I'm just a postman. You're going to have to explain in more detail.'

Mole sighed, frustrated. 'In this copy of *A Tale of Two Cities* are the ingredients to make the enhancers you need – the Mirth. With a cypher, I'll interpret the information and have the Mirth ready in a few hours. With the Mirth I'm making, your hacker will be able to get into anywhere. Your client will still need to acquire a competent enough hacker to help you achieve their goal.'

'Their goal? And what would that be, exactly?'

Mole eyed him suspiciously. 'Are you sure you're the Postman?'

The Postman showed him the badge on his lapel. 'How does the Mirth help? I thought androids used it to get high – stay on the Net longer.'

Mole smiled with superiority. The Postman hated when people did that – just because he wasn't interested in the Net and uploading and Mirth...

'With the right kind of Mirth, hackers can code faster. A lot faster. It enhances the processes inside the CPU.' Mole tapped the side of his head. 'Find the right android, and give them the right kind of Mirth, and an android's CPU can romp like the mind of God.'

The Postman waited for Mole to laugh but he didn't. He was being serious.

'That's Fitzgerald.' Mole said, and showed him another

old book. *The Great Gatsby.* 'Romp like the mind of God. Remarkable isn't it?'

The Postman nodded, unsure what to say.

'I have a name and address for you.' Mole looked at the Postman's tracker. 'I'll send it. You'll need this hacker to get past the firewalls. There's no one else I know who can do it. Not even with the right Mirth.'

'Whose firewalls?'

'Fr.e.dom's,' he said without a pause.

'Fr.e.dom? How the hell can he do that?'

'That's what the Mirth is for.'

The Postman checked his wrist for the name and address.

'Vik. SQ. Gold Zone. But that's one of Fr.e.dom's towers.'

'The hacker works for them.'

'You're serious? Why would he help us?'

'I just supply the Mirth-enhancers and pass on the information. The rest is up to you.' Mole placed the book in a drawer. 'Two hours,' he said, 'maybe three.' Then he disappeared behind a bookshelf.

# FIFTEEN

THE POSTMAN RODE his bike into SQ. All this felt messy and he didn't like messy. He was running around for Stig and waiting for notification from Wan. If either of them found out he was delivering for the other, he'd be in all sorts of trouble. Double the Bits, but double the danger. All the Bits in the world wouldn't do him any good if either of them caught him.

Gold Zone was pretty quiet at that time of night. Fr.e.-dom's programmers lived and worked in this zone. They weren't exactly prisoners, but it amounted to the same thing. How Stig thought he'd get this Vik guy out of there without getting caught was anyone's guess. And even if he could get to him, why would he agree to go with him, anyway?

He pulled up and got off the bike.

'It's a fine night,' a voice from behind said.

It was Angelus.

'What are you doing here?' the Postman asked.

'I'm here to help.'

'This is your pick-up and delivery job? You used Stig again?'

'It's the best and most straightforward way of doing it.'

'Not really a straightforward pick-up, though, is it?'

'Nope.' Angelus, dressed in a long dark-green coat with a hood over his grey hair, pointed to the tallest tower in Gold Zone. 'He's in there.'

'Of course he is.' The tower went up forever, vanishing in a haze of neon-illuminated cloud. 'And how do we get him out of there and back over to WQ?'

'Without being seen,' Angelus said, scanning the road.

'Why didn't you say?'

'You're sarcastic, do you know that?'

Angelus crossed the street, pulling his hood further over his head. The Postman followed, treading through puddles. Angelus walked into an alleyway and stood at the foot of the tower, gazing up.

'He's on floor sixty-three, apartment two.'

'Is that so?'

Angelus pointed as though he was about to start climbing himself. Without acknowledging the Postman, he took something from beneath his coat.

The Postman took a step back. 'Is that what I think it is?'

'Drone-copter.'

'Wait a minute...'

The tube Angelus took from his coat telescoped outwards then expanded into a drone-copter, its four black alloy blades each near a metre in length.

The Postman took another two steps back. 'No way!'

Angelus took no notice and continued to work out where the apartment was above them.

'If you go directly up from this point, you should find his apartment. There's a balcony outside his window.'

'I've seen these things in action.'

'They're perfectly safe.'

Angelus gestured to the handlebars. The drone-copter spluttered.

'This thing is as old as you look.' The Postman stared up at the tower and then through the alleyway to check there was no one around.

'It's reliable.' Angelus pointed upwards. 'You'll have to count the floors. There are no numbers on this side of the building.'

'I told you. No way I'm using this thing.'

Angelus stared at him, sighed and took back the drone-copter. 'No problem. I'll pass on my disappointment to your employer.'

'You mean Stig?'

'I shall inform your employer, who I hear is also a crazy, vengeful murderer, that you did not complete your delivery.'

The postman snatched back the drone-copter. 'What if I use this thing to fly out of Lundun?'

'Good luck outrunning the wall-drones.'

'I might have better odds surviving them than this.' The Postman gazed up the height of the tower, raindrops hitting his face.

'Come with me,' he said to Angelus. 'These things take two easily.'

'They're designed for one.'

'So how do I get down?'

'Take the stairs. Use his password.'

'You've thought of everything, huh?'

'If you stay on this trajectory, and count sixty-three floors, you'll arrive outside his balcony.'

The Postman held the drone-copter above his head and glanced at Angelus. 'Thanks for the advice.'

'Hold tight.'

He stared up through the spinning blades, gripped the

throttle on the handlebar and twisted it. He lifted off the ground and began to count. If he didn't get out of this deal with Stig and Wan soon, he wouldn't last another day.

Thirteen, fourteen, fifteen...

The tower was quiet. He saw lights inside some rooms as he rose, but no one on their balcony.

Twenty-one, twenty-two...

He told himself repeatedly not to look down. That was the trick with these things. A Postman's number one rule: never look down. The drone coughed before speeding up.

Thirty-five, thirty-six...

He passed a woman doing Pilates, no end of androids on their backs hooked up to the Net, and a couple doing it in their living room.

Fifty-nine, sixty...

He slowed down, ready to drop onto the guy's balcony. What the hell was he going to say to him? He manoeuvred over to the balcony and grabbed it with one hand, then climbed over the rail. The drone-copter collapsed when he switched it off so it was small enough to push inside his jacket pocket.

The room on the other side of the window was dark, making it look as though no one was home. Maybe this guy was hooked up to the Net or defragmenting. He checked his wrist. It wasn't long after midnight. A postman had to unlock all manner of doors and locks – they were experts. He took out his digipad and fixed it to the door frame. He concentrated, connecting with the digipad and then with the lock inside the door frame. It was like chasing a mouse through a maze. But he'd had years of practice, and always caught it eventually.

The lock clicked and the door opened.

Taking back the digipad, he waited for a sign that

someone had heard him, but all was quiet on the other side of the door. He pushed it open. The air inside was cooler, filtered and clean. He crept through the apartment. Did anyone actually live here? Maybe he hadn't counted the right number of floors on the way up.

There was a beeping from the bedroom.

He froze, then crept towards the doorway.

The guy was lying on the bed, hooked up to a terminal. The Postman knew one when he saw one: this guy was a Mirth-head. He was out of it, flying sky-high through the Net. Creeping into the room, the Postman reached for his pistol, then thought better of it. If he took this guy out of his high with a pistol pointed at his head, there was no telling what craziness he might unleash.

He powered down the guy's terminal and waited.

A minute later, the guy lurched left and right then sat up straight, gasping for air.

Moving quickly, the Postman covered the guy's mouth. 'Don't say a word. Let me explain.'

A look of terror covered the guy's face. His long, lank hair was drenched with sweat. He was frozen, petrified. Which was understandable.

'Nod if you understand. And I'll move my hand.'

The guy nodded quickly, his eyes wide open.

The Postman moved his hand, ready to put it back if the guy shouted. 'I'm a postman.'

The android's eyes were wide as he came round, scanning the room. 'What happened? I was...'

'Are you Vik?'

He nodded again.

'I need you to come with me.'

'With you? Who are you?'

'I'll explain everything. We need your help with coding.'

Vik smiled as if the Postman had told him a joke. 'I work for Fr.e.dom. There is no coding for anyone else.'

'We don't want you to tell them you're helping us.'

'But I'm not.'

'When you do.'

'I'm not.'

There wasn't a lot the Postman could do unless the guy agreed. There was no way he would make it through the building with a pistol held to the guy's head. 'We can give you all the Mirth you need.'

'I have all I want.' He pointed to a side table strewn with pills.

The Postman considered getting out his pistol and shooting him. Maybe in the arm ... then tell him the next one would be through his head if he didn't go with him. He stood and turned to leave. 'Can I show you something that might change your mind?'

Vik raised an eyebrow, confused. 'Okay ... And if it doesn't, you'll leave?'

'I promise.' He walked out of the room and onto the balcony, the guy following him.

'Look,' he said, pointing down to the small green speck that was Angelus. 'That man can help you get out of this place for good.'

'Out? Why would I want to get out? Fr.e.dom gives me everything I need.'

'But you're a prisoner. You work and live in the same building and you can't go anywhere else.'

'Why would I want to go anywhere? I can go anywhere I want on the Net. One day I'll upload for good. I'm done with this place.'

'All that's bullshit,' the Postman said. 'The Messiah, the New Net – all of it. Don't believe any of it.'

'It's all real,' Vik said, 'believe me. It's real.'

The Postman hesitated. Vik might have been a Mirth-head, but he wasn't stupid; the Postman could see that. The rumours of a Messiah and a New Net, where androids could upload permanently and escape Fr.e.dom's control, were rife. He didn't believe any of it though. It was the latest in a line of fantasies androids invented to cope with the drudgery of living in Lundun under Fr.e.dom's control. The Postman rarely visited the Net, knowing what kind of place it was and how addictive it could be. But there were more and more rumours about androids uploading permanently – leaving their bodies behind – prepared to give it all up to attain a place on the New Net.

'Uploading permanently is illegal,' was all the Postman could say.

Vik shrugged.

'I give up!'

'What are you doing?'

The Postman grabbed Vik's belt and threw him over the balcony so he was hanging onto the rail, yelling at the Postman, who jumped over, activated the drone-copter and dragged Vik down holding his belt with one hand and the drone-copter's handlebar with the other. It stopped them from free-falling, and they glided towards the ground.

Vik was panting and crying when they landed on the pavement.

'I told you it would handle two,' the Postman said to Angelus.

# SIXTEEN

THE POSTMAN, Angelus, and a scared-witless coding Mirth-head walked into a drenched alleyway...

That's how human jokes began. But for the Postman, this was his life.

He stared at Vik, who was quivering in the rain, but spoke to Angelus. 'What now?'

'You go back to the bookshop,' Angelus said.

'How do I get through the tolls?'

'You're a postman. You make deliveries.'

'My parcels don't tend to be shivering, petrified androids who work for Fr.e.dom.'

'We need a box,' Angelus said, scanning the alleyway.

'You're not putting me in a box,' Vik said.

'Your name's Vik,' Angelus said. 'Is that right?'

Vik nodded, huddled up against a wall, trembling.

Angelus crouched next to him. 'We're taking you out of this place. You'll be free.'

'I've told him,' Vik said, pointing at the Postman. 'I don't want to be free.'

Angelus turned to the Postman who pointed up at the

apartment tower.

'That's why we had to take the quick way down.'

Angelus took a deep breath and moved closer to Vik, who leaned away from Angelus, clearly scared.

'You use Mirth?' Angelus asked.

Vik nodded, his gaze flicking back and forth between Angelus and the Postman.

'I know why,' Angelus said. 'Believe me. I know why you do it. The trouble with Mirth, though, is that you become accustomed to it. You need bigger hits each time, until eventually it doesn't work at all.'

There was recognition in Vik's eyes.

'You know what I'm talking about, don't you?' Angelus asked.

Vik's nod was almost imperceptible, but it was there.

'I'm giving you the chance to break into the most protected, the most advanced, the most famous coding ever designed.' Angelus's smile was almost evil. 'Can you imagine the kind of Mirth you'll need to do that? Azure Blue, Lemon Yellow...'

'You have that?' Vik asked, no longer trembling, his eyes open wide.

Angelus nodded. 'And I'm told you have the programming skills.'

Vik was almost bashful as he wiped wet hair from his face. 'With the right Mirth, I can break any code.'

'Even Fr.e.dom's?'

Vik laughed nervously. 'Are you serious?'

Angelus didn't laugh, and his smile was gone. 'Deadly serious.'

Vik glanced at the Postman, maybe asking for suggestions. He didn't have any to offer.

Angelus helped Vik stand. 'You'll be famous. All over the

world.'

'You really have Lemon Yellow Mirth?' Vik asked. 'And Azure Blue?'

Angelus let go of Vik's arm. 'Come with us. I'll show you Mirth the colours of the rainbow.'

There was no need to put Vik in a box. He got on the bike behind the Postman and they set off for EQ, River Zone, and the bookshop, leaving Angelus behind. The tolls were empty and the usual guys were on, who nodded at the Postman as he approached.

The Postman pulled up outside the bookshop. Lola stood in the doorway. He didn't think he'd get to see her again. He couldn't move or speak.

'Postman,' she said. 'It's good to see you.' She motioned for Vik to go into the bookshop. 'You've delivered again, I see.'

Vik walked past Lola into the shop.

'Hey,' she said to the Postman. 'You okay? You've gone a strange colour.'

'Yeah. Fine. What are you doing here? You're human.'

She patted herself all over. 'I am?'

'You know what I mean. It's risky.'

'Relax. No one would believe I'm here, walking about. We're safe.' She took his arm and pulled him inside. 'Come on.'

Seeing her, confused him all over again. He hadn't known Lola for long, but in the time he had, he was pretty sure he'd fallen for her. Which was maybe the most stupid thing he could've done. He followed her into the bookshop and down to the basement.

'Where's Jack?' he asked, a tinge of jealousy in his voice that he couldn't hide.

'He's working over in WQ, Spice Zone, on another lead.'

Vik was already in the basement, peering over the shoulder of a bunch of coders hard at work, off their heads on Mirth.

'This is Mole,' Lola said, introducing the Postman to the bookshop owner he'd met earlier.

'We've met,' he said, nodding at him.

'I didn't think you'd manage it,' Mole said, staring at Vik. 'He's a top-quality coder. The best.'

'He took some convincing. But we got there.'

'You threw me off my balcony,' Vik said without looking at the Postman.

Lola shook off a confused expression.

Vik tore himself away from the other coders. 'What do you want me to do, exactly?'

Lola pointed to an empty seat in front of a terminal. 'We need you to break into Fr.e.dom's coding.'

'You have the Mirth?' Vik asked.

'Nearly. Mole's working on it.'

'What do you want with Fr.e.dom's coding?'

Lola waited, one hand held in the other. For the first time since the Postman had met her, she appeared unsure. 'We're breaking into their records to reset Lundun's Bit debt.'

The room was silent apart from the low hum of the cooling system.

'What?' Vik asked.

'I know it sounds crazy,' Lola said.

'You could say that,' Vik said. 'Or impossible.'

Lola took a deep breath. 'We have information taken straight from Rex's CPU. Imagine it. All debt, for everyone in Lundun, reset, with no surviving records. It would take away Fr.e.dom's control over everyone. We could fight back. It would show androids all around the world that we don't

have to put up with state sponsorship – with huge corporations governing our lives.'

Vik shook his head. 'The firewalls are due for enhance-
ment. The AI system they've developed is far more
advanced than the current system. I've seen it. It will be
impossible to break.'

'Which is why we have to do it before their AI updates
and takes control of the firewalls.'

'That gives us less than six hours.'

Lola bit her bottom lip.

'It can't be done,' Vik said.

Mole walked into the room with vials of Mirth.

Vik saw them and his eyes opened wide. 'Is that …
Scarlet Mirth?'

Mole placed the colourful vials on the table beside the
terminal.

'We can't use that,' the Postman said. 'It'll fry his CPU.'

Vik wasn't listening. Instead, he was wide-eyed, clearly
imagining the high it would give him as he worked the
terminal, diving deeper and deeper into Fr.e.dom's coding.

'We won't need it,' Lola said.

'So why do you have it?'

No one answered.

'When do we start?' Vik asked.

'When you're ready,' Lola said. 'We're going to reset all
Bit accounts to zero, one.'

'Zero, one,' Vik said. 'I like it.' He began typing and swip-
ing. 'Who are you people, anyway?'

'Digital Skin,' the Postman said.

'Digital … you mean … the terrorist group?'

The Postman saw the moment Vik registered who he
was dealing with.

'Oh,' Vik said eventually. 'Fuck.'

# SEVENTEEN

AS MOLE HELPED Vik hook up, the Postman felt his tracker buzz. It was Wan.

'What's wrong?' Lola asked.

'I have a problem. Two problems, actually. I'm caught between two crooks: Stig, the guy you used to get me into this mess, and a guy who's taken over from Zero in WQ, called Wan. He's with the Brotherhood. They both want me delivering for them – thing is, I can't exactly refuse either of them and stay alive too.'

'That *is* a problem.'

'Thanks for the input.'

'I can help. Once this is done we'll help you. I promise.'

'Yeah, well, for now, to keep a head on my shoulders I have to do this job.'

'Will you come back?' she asked.

'My job's done. I've delivered. When you're done with the coder, you help me find Blood and Bone. That was the deal.'

'Help us. We could use you on our side.'

He couldn't stop thinking about how lucky Jack was. It

was torture, knowing the two of them were together. And Jack was him ... or he was Jack ... or however it worked.

'I'll see how long the drop-off takes.'

'Come back,' she said.

Sometimes, for a split second, he'd forget there was another him, a human version.

The pick-up wasn't far away – close by in River Zone, EQ. He took his bike and weaved through the early morning drizzle towards the address. It hit him that if Lola and Vik pulled it off, all the Bits he'd saved for his retirement would vanish. It would work out well for all those with nothing, or who owed Fr.e.dom a small fortune – which, to be fair, was most of Lundun. But he'd lose everything he'd worked so hard for.

He pulled up outside the pick-up, strapped on his bag, checked his pistols and headed inside. It was another tower. He spent most of his days making his way up and down these towers. He needed an apartment on the fourth floor, so there was no need to take the lift. Apartment six. He knocked on the door and stared at the camera above, nodded, then showed the badge on his lapel.

'Postman,' he said to the door. Finally, it opened to reveal a woman dressed in an all-in-one leopard-print jumpsuit. 'That's some outfit you have on.'

'It's not an outfit,' she said, as if she'd had to explain a million times before. She walked into her apartment and he followed her, narrowing his eyes. She was right. It was some kind of all-over tattoo.

'You're naked?'

'Does it make you uncomfortable?' She stooped to move boxes in the corner of the room.

'Well...'

'You're a postman; you must see all kinds of things.'

'I guess so.'

She handed over a shoebox wrapped in leopard-print paper, the same pattern that covered her body.

He turned the box over in his hands. 'Stylish.'

She raised a hand like a claw and pretended to swipe at him like a cat. 'Meow.'

'I should go...' He headed back down the stairs and got on the bike. Leopard-woman was right – Lundun shouldn't surprise him. But it did … every now and then.

The address for the drop-off came through. Still in River Zone, EQ, which made it easier. The guys at the tolls hardly ever stopped a postman, but still, it was better they didn't see him delivering stuff like this. Not that he knew what it was. He could guess … but he never knew for sure. That's the way he liked it. A postman's number one rule: don't ask too many questions.

He knew all about the apartment block he was headed for. EQ, like every other quadrant, had its glitterati – its notorious. There was a bohemian scene in River Zone, and the androids on this scene revered the human equivalent of the same movement of the twentieth century. They enjoyed slumming it in EQ instead of living it up in luxury in NQ. Some things the Postman just didn't understand – like why women tattooed their entire bodies in leopard print. Or these bohemians – why did they read human novels, exchange human paintings, listen to human music … even dress like them?

Pulling up outside the apartment tower, he strapped on his bag and peered up at the tower. He could see what he was dealing with from there. He sighed heavily and entered the building.

Floor seventy-seven, apartment seven.

'Delivery!' he shouted, banging on the door.

Eventually the door opened.

'Delivery for Bo,' he said, stepping inside.

There was no clue from outside what this place was like on the inside. It was huge. There must have been twenty apartments, all knocked through to make one vast dance floor. Music played – acoustic guitar with a solemn-sounding voice singing over the top of it. He didn't know what the twentieth century had to moan about, but this guy singing was definitely sad about how the times were changing.

'The Postman!' a guy shouted, walking over to him, his arms raised as though he was ready to hug him. He wore a blue dress, had long blue hair down to his waist, and huge wooden beads around his neck. 'I still love getting a delivery.'

'Bo?' the Postman asked. 'Delivery for you.'

'Magnificent,' Bo said, taking the leopard-print shoebox. 'Isn't she a doll?' He turned to shout to everyone. 'Look. At. This. Paper!' No one took any notice, but that didn't dampen his spirits.

'Just need recognition,' the Postman said, offering his wrist.

'Wait a minute,' Bo said. 'You must have a drink before you go. What's your name?'

The Postman was in no mood to explain, so pretended not to hear him. He hated it when they did this. They thought they were doing him a favour – not recognising the delivery until he'd had a break or they'd thanked him. He didn't have the time.

'I really need to—'

And Bo was off, waving for him to follow. He reached a long settee next to the dance floor, on which around fifty people swayed and sang, and flopped down. He placed both hands on the shoebox. 'You must try one of these.'

The Postman didn't sit down. That would have only encouraged him. Never sit down. Number one rule for a postman.

Bo unwrapped and opened the box. He took out a heap of blister packs of Mint-green Mirth.

'It's a new variety,' he said, holding one of the packs close to his face. 'I've been told they give you a gentle, euphoric high that accentuates the appreciation of the arts: music, paintings, literature ... all of it. *And* they freshen your breath.' He stared at the pills, grinning.

The Postman checked his wrist. 'Look, buddy, I really need your recognition so I can—'

Bo wasn't listening. It was useless. He took one of the pills, throwing back his head and hair in an exaggerated manner.

'Here,' he said, handing one to the Postman.

'Will you recognise the delivery if I take it?'

Bo nodded, his eyes on the pill between the Postman's finger and thumb.

The Postman took it, threw it into his mouth, and swallowed. He'd taken this kind of pill a thousand times. They didn't do a lot for him. They were a weak formulation used to trick guys like these at this party that they were slumming it in a more sophisticated way.

He held out his wrist, Bo blinked, and Wan was notified that the delivery was done. *That should keep him off his back for a while.*

Now, Bo had an arm around the Postman's shoulder and was walking him over to the enormous wall on the other side of the apartment. It was covered in paintings.

'Look at them,' he said, one arm embracing the Postman, the other sweeping across the wall.

'Are they human?' the Postman asked, knowing the answer.

'Most of them.'

'Most?'

Bo ushered him along the line and pointed to a painting of a fuzzy-looking guy. 'Edmond de Belamy,' Bo said, as if in awe. He turned to the Postman. 'Have you heard of it?'

'Can't say I have. Who is it?'

'It was the first notable piece of art created using AI. It sold for over $400,000 in 2018.'

'Was that a lot?'

'It was for a piece of art made by an AI.'

'Typical,' the Postman said.

'What?'

'Doesn't it say something that the first work of art by an AI was of a human?'

Bo's shoulders fell. 'Maybe. But it was the start of a new digital movement. That was not really AI the way we know it can be. It was more an algorithm. But an important moment all the same.' Bo showed the Postman along the massive wall of paintings. 'Picasso, Monet, Gauguin, Bacon, van Gogh, Cezanne. This one belongs to...' He broke off and turned on the spot, scanning all around. Bo moved closer. 'The Messiah.'

The Postman was hearing about this guy more and more.

'You know him?'

Bo arranged his dress on his shoulders and gazed at him seriously. 'My dear, I shouldn't have said anything.' An expression of pride coloured his face. 'But he is a dear friend.'

'Have you met him?'

'Once.' Bo placed a hand on the postman's arm. 'He is a remarkable android.' Bo closed his eyes and lifted his head to face the ceiling. 'Truly remarkable.'

The Postman turned again to the paintings and had an idea. If he was going to find Blood and Bone, he would no doubt need Bits to do it. He needed to hang on to them some way. 'Are these worth a lot?'

Bo's eyes narrowed on him as though waiting to be told he was joking. 'My dear postman, they're priceless.'

'But if you had to put a price on them?'

Bo shook his head and smirked. 'They're priceless.'

'What about ten thousand Bits?'

Bo's face changed. He was no longer smirking. 'Which one do you want?'

It could be the effect of the Mint-green Mirth, or the fact that at any moment Bits wouldn't be worth the electricity it took to illuminate a digit on his tracker, but the Postman was soon the proud owner of two Picassos, a Francis Bacon, and a Seurat.

'You're sure these will keep their value?' he asked.

Bo ignored his question. 'Where does a postman get all these Bits?'

'I stay busy.' He pointed to the paintings – *his* paintings – up on the wall. 'And you'll keep them for me. For now?'

'Of course. They're safe here with me.'

The Postman walked over to the door, looking back at the row of paintings on the wall. After this, he thought, Vik had better pull it off.

# EIGHTEEN

AS SOON AS he left Bo's apartment, he was thinking about Lola. He was always going to go back to the bookshop. On the way, his tracker buzzed with messages from Stig and Wan. He really couldn't keep delivering for both of them. It wouldn't work. But there was no way he could turn down work from either of them. So, he ignored both.

In the basement of the bookshop, Vik had already taken the Azure Blue Mirth and was making headway into Fr.e.-dom's code.

'This might actually work,' Mole said.

'Where'd you go?' Lola asked the Postman.

'To buy some art.'

She frowned. 'What?'

'Never mind. Long story.' He checked his wrist again and saw Stig was asking for him. 'I need to make some calls. Stig and Wan.'

'Ah,' Lola said, biting her bottom lip. 'We might have a problem there.'

He felt cold and hot at the same time, his stomach flipping. 'A problem?'

'Angelus thinks they got wind of us taking Vik from under Fr.e.dom's nose, and they want answers. They're not the only ones.'

'Answers? Do they know what we're doing?'

'I don't think so. But I guess they'll soon work out something's going on.'

'I need the Lemon Yellow,' Vik said. 'I've gone as deep as I can.'

Mole glanced at Lola questioningly.

Lola nodded. 'Do it.'

The Postman knew it was going to happen, but now he knew both Stig and Wan would be looking for answers, the only way out would be to get out of Lundun. 'How much longer?' the Postman asked her.

She shrugged. 'We're not sure.'

'You're very calm. Considering.'

'Not a lot I can do.'

There was a loud knock from upstairs.

'It's the bookshop door,' Mole said, injecting Vik's forearm with Mirth.

'Are you closed?' the Postman asked.

Mole raised the syringe and pointed it at Vik. 'What do you think?'

'I'll handle it,' Lola said.

'No.' The Postman stopped her. 'We can't risk them suspecting you're human. I'll go.'

He took a deep breath and headed up the stairs, making sure the doors were closed behind him. It couldn't be Wan or Stig; they wouldn't have made it through the tolls and out of WQ themselves. But they could always employ others to do their dirty work. They were certainly used to doing that.

There were two dark figures on the other side of the

glass door. He took off his postman's jacket and hid it behind the counter. He unlocked the front door and opened it.

'We're looking for Mole,' one guy said. He was serious-looking, with a shaved head, the same as the guy next to him.

'He's not available at the moment. Can I help you? We're closed but—'

'Who are you?' the guy asked, walking into the shop, forcing the Postman to walk backwards.

'I help with the books,' he said, pointing at the bookcase beside him.

The androids glanced at one another. It was obvious they didn't believe a word he was saying.

'Stig sent us,' the other guy said.

'Who?'

'Stig. He wants us to speak to Mole. So if you could run and get him...' The big guy stared at the Postman like there should have been an 'or else' at the end of his request.

'Like I said, he's otherwise engaged.'

The two of them edged closer, not saying a word.

The Postman swallowed loudly. 'We had a beautiful copy of Charles Dickens' *A Tale of Two Cities* in earlier. Maybe I could interest you in—'

The guy on the right stepped on the Postman's toes, stopping him from backing away any further. He was tall and as wide as a utility-bot.

'You're ... on my toes.'

'Get. Mole,' the other guy snarled.

'No problem. If you could just...'

The guy took his weight off his foot and the Postman stood up straight. He needed the colours to come to him, the many worlds, but they weren't there. What was the use in having the ability Angelus described if he couldn't call on it when needed?

'For a big guy, you have tiny feet,' the Postman said, staring down at them.

The guy looked down too. It was his chance.

The Postman gave the guy who stood on his toes an uppercut, sending him sprawling. The other guy reached for his pistol, giving the Postman the chance to get in the first blow. He kicked him in the stomach, and his pistol flew into the air. It landed and skidded beneath the counter. He turned to the first guy he'd hit, but it was too late. The other guy punched him in the head. His punch meant business. The Postman fell to the ground, his head spinning. He grabbed the pistol from his pocket and shot at something moving in front of him. There was a cry of pain and then two more gunshots that weren't his. He waited for the pain, but all he felt was a throb from the punch in the head. All movement stopped and he heard a familiar voice.

'Postman. You okay?'

It was Lola.

'Where are they?' he asked.

'I shot them.'

'No,' he said. 'We can't kill them. Stig will know.'

'We're close,' she said. 'We can't risk anyone finding out what we're doing. They'll stop us.'

She helped him stand. 'That looks bad,' she said, wincing at the cut on the side of his head. He reached to touch it and felt the alloy beneath the ripped skin.

'I'm fine. We need to get out of here. Stig will send more of them.'

'We can't. We have to wait until Vik resets the Bit debt.'

'You don't understand. Stig will send an army. If he

thinks we're up to something, which we are, he'll be on us in minutes.'

Lola scanned the shop. 'Mole says there's a back way out of here that no one knows about. The shop front is the only way in. We just have to defend this door until Vik does it.'

'We don't stand a chance.'

She headed to the stairs and down to the basement. He followed her. Vik was still hooked up.

'He's close,' Mole said. 'What was all that noise up there?'

'We're going to have company real soon,' the Postman told him.

'Company? That doesn't sound good. Are my books going to be okay?'

'We need pistols,' Lola said, walking back and forth, collecting pistols and rifles from her duffel bag and Mole's collection.

'Lola says there's another way out,' the Postman said to Mole. 'Where is it?'

Mole looked worried. 'Should we be using it?'

'*I'm* using it,' the Postman said. 'Where is it?'

'You can't,' Lola said. 'We're close.'

'Sorry. Not my fight.' He turned to Mole, who was clearly more than ready to make a run for it with him. 'Show me the way out.'

'It's through to the shop next door, then up a fire escape and across the rooftops.'

'Good,' the Postman said. 'Let's go.' He held Lola's arm. 'You're coming with us. It's useless staying here.'

'No,' she snapped, snatching her arm away. 'I'm staying. I need to stop them getting to Vik.'

'He won't do it in time. It's too late.'

'Not if we give him the Scarlet Mirth,' Mole said.

'We can't,' the Postman said. 'It'll kill him. On top of the Mirth he's already had, it'll fry his CPU.'

Lola stared at the syringe filled with a deep red liquid. He could see she was thinking of using it.

'We have to go,' the Postman said. 'We can try it again another time.'

'But there won't be another time.' Lola stared at the vial of Scarlet Mirth. 'Once the new firewalls are up, we'll be a million miles behind them again. It has to be now.'

'I'm taking these books,' Mole said, pushing some chosen ones into a bag. 'I'm not hanging around here. Are you coming?'

The Postman stared at Lola.

'Go,' she said. 'I wouldn't blame you.'

'What about Vik?'

'He's worth too much to them alive. He'll be fine.'

'Are you coming?' Mole asked, hugging a bag filled with books, glancing the way they needed to go.

Lola smiled and left to climb the stairs to the shop front, carrying an arsenal of weapons.

Mole was waiting for him.

The door at the top of the stairs opened and closed, and Lola was gone.

'I can't leave her here,' the Postman said.

'Suit yourself.' Mole left, followed by the other remaining coders. Finally, the only sound in the basement was the whir of the terminal Vik was using.

The Postman's wrist buzzed with a message from Stig. 'You're dead, Postman.'

# NINETEEN

THE POSTMAN ARRIVED next to Lola. 'What's the plan?'

She didn't even flinch.

'You knew I'd stay, didn't you?'

She loaded and activated a rifle, smacking it on the floor in front of him. 'I know you.'

What she meant was she knew Jack, which was the same as knowing him, he guessed. He pointed to the dead guys stretched out on the shop floor. 'Stig will know from their readouts I'm here and that I'm helping you.'

She looked concerned. 'Sorry.'

'I guess retirement really is out of the picture.'

'If Vik pulls this off, everything will change. Lundun will be a different place.'

'How?'

'I don't know exactly. It could be messy for a while.'

She lined up the rest of the pistols and rifles behind the counter.

'Are you sure we're doing the right thing? Resetting the Bits? What if people lose it and start killing each other?'

She froze and stared at one of the pistols. 'I've given it a lot of thought. The truth is, I don't know what will happen. But what I do know is, we can't let things carry on as they are.'

'It will cause mayhem,' he said.

'Like I say, I've given it a lot of thought.'

'And you still think it's the right thing to do?'

She handed him a rifle. 'I think it's the only thing we *can* do.'

He checked the rifle was loaded.

'We'll give Vik ten more minutes,' she said. 'If he's not there, I'm giving him the Scarlet Mirth.'

'It'll kill him.'

She gazed at him side-on. 'Let's hope he makes it inside the firewalls.'

He was pretty sure she'd do it, too. Again, it made him question her view of androids – would she have considered doing it to a human?

Lola moved from behind the counter and pushed one of the bookcases with a shoulder, but it didn't move. 'Help me move this.'

It was hard to believe, considering, but he felt bad for Mole and all the old books. He was no fan of human books, but still, it felt kind of wasteful. He helped Lola push over the bookcases, making a barrier between the rear of the shop and the way in. They hid behind the counter, each holding a rifle.

'I haven't had a chance to thank you,' she said.

'For what?'

'For trying to get Lola out of that place. I know you didn't want to leave her there.'

'Leaving her there didn't feel right. But she insisted.'

'It was important. She knew that.'

'She knew she was going to die, didn't she?'

Lola nodded, her eyes sad.

'And you know too?' he asked her. 'You're prepared to die for this, huh?'

She nodded again. 'We have to make a stand. It's not just humankind that's in trouble. Fr.e.dom controls millions of androids, the same way other huge corporations control androids around the world.'

'You can't tell me you're fighting for androids, too?'

She narrowed her eyes. 'I am. I fight against all totalitarian regimes. There's no reason androids and humans can't live together.'

The way she spoke made him think about the poem Mole had shown him – Blake's 'London'. Nonetheless, the Postman could think of many reasons why humans and androids wouldn't be able to live side by side. But he kept them to himself.

There was a banging at the shop door.

'Postman!' someone shouted.

'How long do we have to keep them here?' he asked Lola.

'As long as it takes.' The door to the basement was closed. 'When we have to, we'll go downstairs and shut that door behind us to slow them down. It's pretty heavy. Then we'll protect Vik until it's done.'

'For a human, you're pretty methodical.'

'For an android, you're a bit of a softie.'

'I'm not a softie.'

She smiled and lifted her head to peer over the counter.

'Postman!' one of Stig's men shouted. 'Time to come out!'

'Do they think I'm just going to walk out there with my hands in the air?'

He was about to raise his head when they opened fire, smashing every pane of glass at the front of the shop, which was now filled with a confetti of shredded books. There was the sound of them kicking in the door and windows, then more gunfire.

'Ready?' Lola asked.

He wasn't, but nodded anyway.

Lola was first to go. She lifted her head, a pistol in each hand, shooting through the haze of destruction. He rolled to the other side of the counter and pulled the trigger on his rifle. It took three shots to get his eye in and to work out what was in front of him. He took out one of them trying to get through a window, then turned the rifle on a huge guy stumbling over one of the bookcases. The Postman ducked back behind the counter to reload and saw Lola doing the same.

His head throbbed, then everything fractured. Colours fanned out before his eyes. Time slowed down and he saw the many worlds Angelus had described. Now he knew the theory behind it, they looked different somehow – more distinct, or defined. The reds and oranges shifted first, each one showing him and Lola dead, inert on the ground. But in yellow, he saw Lola closing the door to the basement, heading away from danger.

'We won't last much longer,' he shouted, choosing the yellow world. 'There are more of them outside the shop. Did you see them?'

Lola jumped up again and fired. For a human, she was one hell of a shot.

He followed her, shooting a guy who was about to jump over the counter towards them.

'I see them!'

Lola dodged between bookcases, firing as she did. He followed her, taking out another guy on his way.

'Go to the basement,' he said.

Lola edged towards the door.

'We need to get behind that door,' he said. 'Then if they get through to the staircase, we can pick them off one at a time. Go!' he shouted, covering her retreat.

He took a deep breath and followed.

She shut the door and bolted it. He thumped the door to test its strength.

'It won't last long,' he said. His head throbbed as if it was being crushed from both sides.

'You okay?' Lola asked, leading him down the stairs and into the room where Vik was hooked up to the terminal.

'Postman?' she asked.

'I'm fine ... I'm fine.' He held his head and focused on the screen Vik was working on.

'He's nearly there,' Lola said.

It was hard to believe, but Vik was deep inside Fr.e.dom's code and might actually do it.

'We have to wait until he's done,' she said. 'It's now or never.'

There was a banging at the door. Then gunshots.

'Hurry!' Lola shouted, as though Vik could hear her.

'It's no good,' the Postman said, grabbing Lola's arm. 'We have to go.' His head throbbed again, making him stumble, everything spinning.

'No!' She grabbed the syringe of Scarlet Mirth.

'You can't!' he shouted, trying to take it from her. She pushed him away, stopped, and stared at the syringe, then at the door. More gunfire.

'Don't do it,' he said, again holding his head in his hands. The spectrum he'd seen was taking its toll.

She held the syringe next to Vik's arm. 'You don't understand what this could do for everyone in Lundun. All that debt – gone in an instant.'

'You wouldn't do it if he was human.'

She frowned, annoyed. 'I'd do it to myself if I had to.'

There was a crash and the door burst open.

The Postman fell backward, his rifle thrown behind him.

The sound of gunfire.

Lola grabbing his arm.

He couldn't see straight ... couldn't think.

He stood, grabbed his rifle and fired. Bodies fell down the stairs and landed in a heap at the bottom.

'Hurry!' Lola shouted from behind, pulling his arm. 'This way!'

They ran through a corridor then climbed a ladder. Lola held his hand and pulled him up out of a small opening. He was outside. It was raining and the air was cool.

'What happened?'

'It's okay,' Lola said. 'We're out. We made it.'

'Vik? Where's Vik?'

'I don't know.'

'We have to go back. We can't leave him there.'

'Stop!' she said. 'We can't go back. It's too late.'

'What do you mean?'

Lola walked to the edge of the roof and pointed to the glimmering horizon, to the lights of the Lundun skyline.

'Look,' she said.

'What?'

'That's Lundun on the brink of a change unlike any in history – android or human.'

'He did it?'

She had tears in her eyes.

'Did you give...'

Her expressions and eyes told him not to ask again. So he didn't. He didn't want to hear her say what he already knew.

## TWENTY

LOLA LED the way through EQ and River Zone until they reached the Thames.

'Down here.' She pointed to a set of brick steps that led beneath the bridge.

They hid, backs to the wall.

'Check your Bits,' she said, nodding at his tracker. 'We need to know it's worked.'

He checked his account and showed Lola. It was all gone. Not that there had been much left after he'd bought the paintings.

'Zero, one.' She covered her mouth. 'Vik did it.'

He stared at his wrist.

Then she was holding him, kissing him. He kissed her back but didn't understand.

She let him go. 'Jack, we did it!'

He stared at her, then touched his lips with two fingers. She'd kissed him ... a human had kissed him. But she'd called him Jack.

'This will change everything,' she said, seemingly unmoved by their kiss.

The sound of drones and sirens blared across the bridge above.

'We need to get back to the others,' she said. 'Is your bike close?'

He was still in a daze. 'It's outside the bookshop. We can't risk it.'

'We need a bike.'

He walked beneath the bridge and stared up at the city skyline. There were drones everywhere, and fires too, smoke billowing upward.

'What's happening?'

Lola was beside him. 'I don't know. But I'm guessing it's because of what we've done. They're free. They're all free!'

It was ironic. Now *he* was anything but free. Stig would be searching for him, ready to hunt him down. Wan too, most likely, when he found out the Postman was the reason his Bits had gone missing.

'If we find a bike,' he said, 'I can start it.'

He led the way out from under the bridge and headed in the opposite direction, to where the drones were making their way above the streets.

'There,' Lola said, pointing to a bar.

He took out his digipad and fastened it to the handle-bars of a bike.

'What now?' she asked.

'We wait. The digipad will hack it.'

'Do all postmen get one of those?'

'Only the ones who work for criminals.'

The keypad blinked and bleeped and the bike started. He got on with Lola behind, the bike bouncing under their weight. He twisted the throttle and set off in the direction the drones were flying.

They weaved through abandoned self-drivers and bikes.

There were androids everywhere, celebrating. Drones hovered above, issuing warnings, but no one took any notice. At the centre of River Zone were thousands of androids throwing missiles at police drones, many of which were searching for cover.

Once they were out of the centre of River Zone, then EQ, it was easy going. Lola held on to him. Even now, as Lundun burned, all he thought about was Lola holding and kissing him.

The tolls were abandoned, and they flashed straight through into NQ. The androids there were not going to like what had happened. Most of the androids who owned Bits lived in NQ.

They reached the border of Lundun and his tracker buzzed. The cabin came into view and he took the bike off-road, pulling up outside the cabin. Lola jumped off and ran inside. The Postman followed and they took the lift down. When the doors opened, they were greeted with cheers.

Lola ran into Jack's embrace and kissed him. The Postman watched her kissing him and remembered what it was like.

This really was insane.

'You did it,' Angelus said, arriving beside him.

'I guess so.'

'You don't sound too happy.'

'I still don't know if I should be happy or not. What if people get hurt? It'll be our fault.'

'You helped set them free. You can't control what they do with their freedom.'

'Control. That's an interesting word.'

Lola was still kissing Jack.

'That was all you,' Angelus said. 'He had nothing to do with it. You made your own choices. You know that, right?'

'If you say so.'

'You're one of us now.'

'I should be retired.'

'Retire? And do what?'

'Maybe write the great android epic poem.'

Angelus shrugged. 'Someone's got to.'

# TWENTY-ONE

HE TOOK the bike back through WQ and Jewel Zone to his apartment. Things were crazy – he didn't think anyone would notice him. Androids were burning WQ to the ground. There were no Fr.e.dom drones left – they'd been shot down, leaving debris scattered across the streets. He chicaned through the wreckage on the way back to his apartment.

He left the bike a hundred metres from his apartment tower and headed to the back and the fire escape. Inside the tower, like outside on the streets, there was yelling, loud music and cheering. He had no idea what was going to happen to Lundun but, whatever happened, he figured it was going to be messy.

It was hard work, but he took the stairs up to his floor, all the time looking out for trouble. If he could make it in and out of his apartment with no one spotting him, he'd be lucky.

His apartment was at the end of the hallway. No sign of anyone. He took his time, pistols at the ready, and crept down the corridor. His door was open. He braced himself.

Who had got there before him? A pistol in each hand, he entered, sweeping the apartment.

'You can drop them,' someone said.

The Postman pointed the pistols towards the voice. From the next room, Archer appeared, his hands raised.

The Postman lowered his pistols and puffed out a relieved breath. 'What the hell are you doing here?'

'I was worried about you. I've not seen you around.'

He pushed his pistols into his pockets. 'I'm fine.'

'What's been going on? Did you have anything to do with all this?'

'With what?'

Archer walked to the window and pointed to the chaos in the street below.

'Why would you think that?'

'I hear things. Such as you helping Digital Skin carry out a terrorist attack on Fr.e.dom's Bit system.'

He hated lying to Archer, so it was usually best to say nothing.

'Do you know what they found at that bookshop?' Archer asked. 'In EQ, River Zone?'

The Postman knew exactly what they'd found, but again it was best to say nothing.

'Among the bodies was a guy who'd hacked Fr.e.dom's code.'

The Postman wanted to ask if he was alive, but didn't want to risk giving himself away.

Archer stared at him, waiting. 'He was dead,' he said eventually.

The Postman tried to keep his face impassive.

'He'd taken a deadly dose of Mirth – enhanced.'

The Postman thought about Lola holding the needle. *What was she thinking?*

'They tell me it was the only way he could do it. Without it, he'd never have got deep enough into the coding. He was a remarkable coder by all accounts, but to do what he was trying to do, he needed powerful Mirth. A real waste of talent.'

'That's tragic.'

Archer edged closer. 'I don't know what's going on with you. But I can only look out for you so much.'

'I didn't ask you to look out for me.'

Archer stared him dead in the eyes. For a writer, he was fearsome.

'Yeah, well, I'm doing it anyway.'

The Postman couldn't deal with Archer so he moved through his apartment, collecting the things he wanted to take with him.

'Where are you going?' Archer asked.

'You've seen this place. It's gone crazy. I need to get some space for a while until it all blows over.'

'Blows over?' Archer said. 'This is big. I can't see Lundun recovering and being the way it was before. Times are changing.'

It reminded the Postman of the song he'd heard in Bo's apartment where his art investments hung on the wall. At least, he hoped they still hung on the wall. Who knew what was happening?

He filled a duffel bag with his things.

Archer's tone changed, as if ready to share bad news. 'I've been researching the terrorist group you told me about: Blood and Bone.'

'What about them?'

'You ever wonder what happened to them?'

'They blew themselves up.'

'I know you're going after them – whoever's left, anyway.'

The Postman ignored the comment and continued filling his bag.

'You can't kill an idea,' Archer said. 'You know that, right? Humans want Lundun back. They see it as their rightful home. You can't catch that idea and lock it away. The name of the terrorist group that killed the people we loved has gone, but the idea, maybe even the humans behind it, are still alive.'

He stopped packing. Archer was staring at the floor. The Postman had seen him like this before – his anger simmering.

'Be careful,' Archer said.

'What do you mean?'

'I know you've been with them. With Digital Skin.'

If Archer told anyone, the Postman was a goner.

'I don't know what you're talking about, Arch.'

Archer's face didn't change. 'Because of what we've been through, and because of how much you've helped me, I'll give you fair warning. I'm coming after Digital Skin. If that means I have to go through you, so be it.'

The Postman stared into his eyes and saw how serious he was.

'I'm not fooling about. And there's something else you should know.' Archer's face softened. 'Those people – Digital Skin – they were once Blood and Bone. They're the same group. I want to get even with them as much as you do.'

The Postman's hands froze and he held his breath. Even though he didn't want to believe it, Archer's face told him he was telling the truth.

'You're wrong.'

'They're human. And they want to take back Lundun. Don't let them fool you into believing they want to help us –

to help androids.' He pointed outside again. 'Look – are you telling me that what they've done is helping us?'

'They're free. All of them. What androids do with that freedom is up to them.'

'Wake up! You're smarter than this.'

The Postman went through what Archer was telling him. Lola and Jack were members of Digital Skin, which had once been Blood and Bone, the group Angelus said Mia was a member of.

It couldn't be true.

He remembered Lola holding the Scarlet Mirth, ready to give to Vik. He thought he'd stopped her. She'd used the Mirth knowing it would kill him. The way the Postman felt about her was clouding his judgement. He thumped his head. She was human, like the rest of them; she didn't care about him or any other androids.

'Let me show you something,' Archer said.

'Hang on.' Grabbing a bottle of Grit, the Postman unscrewed the lid and downed the little that remained. He recalled Mia walking away from him, towards the station. He'd seen Lola – or her shadow – that day. She had been there. He let the empty bottle of Grit drop to the floor. In time with the bottle hitting the ground, outside was another explosion, followed by cheering.

'That stuff won't help,' Archer said, leading the way out of the apartment door and into the stairwell.

'Where are we going?' the Postman asked.

'Come with me. You need to see something.'

The Postman didn't like the tone of Archer's voice. It sounded as if he was about to tell him something that would change everything. Again.

## TWENTY-TWO

AT THE END of the hallway, several floors above the Postman's apartment, Archer pointed to a door. 'Can you open it?'

'Why?'

'I'll show you.'

The Postman took his digipad from his pocket and fastened it to the door beside the lock, then synced with it. The lock wasn't much good and the door opened quickly.

'What are we doing here?' the Postman asked.

Archer didn't say anything as he pushed open the door and walked inside. The Postman followed.

There were bodies all over the floor, on settees, chairs, tables, and worktops.

'What *is* this?' the Postman asked.

'They've uploaded,' Archer said, stepping over bodies, walking further into the apartment.

The Postman knew of androids uploading permanently, had even seen some of the bodies left behind. But he'd not seen anything on this scale before.

'Have you heard of the Messiah?' Archer asked.

The Postman was losing patience with talk of a Messiah. 'It's all a fantasy.'

Archer stopped in the middle of the room, surrounded by bodies. 'He has a following. And it's growing.'

'They've all uploaded?' the Postman asked. 'Permanently?'

Archer nodded.

'All of them? Why would they do that?'

Archer didn't answer, simply took in the bodies at his feet.

It was a foolish question, and the Postman knew it. The question should have been, why *wouldn't* an android want to upload? The Net was an infinitely better place for androids than Lundun. Inside the Net, androids could be who they wanted to be.

The Postman stepped over the bodies then stopped. He recognised one of the androids.

'Do you know her?' Archer asked.

He stooped to look at her more closely. 'Yeah. I know her.' Her body was completely still. 'Harriet was a friend of Mia's – a good friend.'

Archer was moving around the room.

'She had real dogs for a while,' the Postman said. 'Even after they were banned. Mia helped her hide them from Fr.e.dom, but they caught up with her eventually. She wasn't the same after that.'

'Did they replace them? The dogs?'

The postman stared at Harriet, waiting for her eyes to open and for her to acknowledge him. But the longer he stared at her face, the more remote that idea became. There was nothing there; she was gone for good.

'No. She didn't want the replacements.'

The Postman stood, took one last look at Harriet, then walked back towards the door.

Archer followed him. 'More and more androids are uploading.'

'How?'

Archer picked up an empty pill box. 'Sky-blue Mirth. If you can get hold of some, and are lucky enough for the Messiah to find you, a permanent place in the New Net can be yours.'

'Do Fr.e.dom not know this is happening?'

'If they do, they're not stopping it.'

'It doesn't make any sense,' the Postman said.

Archer sighed loudly. 'No. It doesn't. But androids are leaving Lundun behind, even if it means leaving their body behind too.'

'Is he a real android? The Messiah?'

Archer shrugged. 'I don't know. He or she could be an android, it could be a group of androids. But whoever it is, they're giving androids a place to escape to. We're told that Fr.e.dom built the walls to keep androids safe from humans. But androids are trapped inside this fortress, inside these walls. The only way out is to upload. The Messiah gives androids that opportunity.' Archer arranged his long coat, fastening it up to his chin. 'This Messiah, whoever he or she might be, is fighting back.'

The Postman stepped out into the hallway. Being inside the apartment with so many cold and still bodies was too eerie.

Archer arrived in the hallway after him. 'Be careful who you make friends with.' He paused, tipped his hat, then walked down the hallway towards the lift.

The Postman looked back into the room towards Harriet. He imagined her on the Net somewhere, a pack of dogs following her. There were so many androids who were better off on the Net than in Lundun. But it wouldn't be long before Fr.e.dom figured out what was happening. Chances were they already knew, and were manipulating it in some way to suit their own ends. He left the apartment and headed for the stairwell, going over all the questions he had for Lola.

He had no control over it – the hatred he had for humans returned.

# TWENTY-THREE

TWO DAYS LATER, from high up on a hill, the Postman watched the first tower falling. Then, carried on a gust of wind, came a low roar as the second and third towers fell. Within seconds, all five Fr.e.dom towers in Gold Zone, SQ, were gone, replaced by plumes of debris and dust. The Lundun skyline would never be the same again.

The Postman picked up and read one of the leaflets scattered across the street telling the employees of Fr.e.dom, who lived in those towers, what was about to happen. He didn't know how many would have heeded the warning.

'Fr.e.dom won't survive this,' Angelus said. 'Not in Lundun. We've done it.'

The dust from the destruction of the towers reached them on the WQ border.

'You've created a power vacuum,' the Postman said, eyes still on the horizon where the towers should have been. 'Who knows what we'll end up with, or who will claim power? What if it's the Brotherhood?'

'That is up to us,' Angelus said. 'Androids must make sure whoever replaces them is just and righteous.'

The trouble with androids like Angelus, the Postman thought, was that they had adopted humanity's idealism. Deep in his make-up was the belief that androids could be good. The truth was, when it came down to it, goodness was a virtue for those who could afford it. He didn't believe that the desire to survive always trumped goodness in androids, as it did in humans. Even now, after everything humanity's history had shown them, there were androids like Angelus who saw the possibility of a utopia.

'You said Lola would be here,' he said.

'She'll be here soon.' Angelus turned away from the destruction.

'I need to talk to her.'

'About what?'

The Postman pointed to the clouds of dust. 'About this, about her connection to the terrorist group who killed Mia, about injecting Vik with Mirth...'

Angelus walked away.

'Hey! I'm talking to you.'

Angelus stopped. 'Lola's brave. There are things you don't know about her.' He closed and then opened his eyes slowly. 'Her methods might be direct, but they're effective. And right now, we need that.'

The Postman pointed to the skyline. 'I've seen that for myself.'

'But her motives are, and always have been, good.'

'I've heard that before, too. How many acts of barbarism throughout history have been done in the name of what is "good"?'

'It's not like that.'

'And how many of those people would have said the same?'

'Then help us. If you don't think what we're doing benefits androids and humans alike, then help us.'

'I wouldn't know what to do for the benefit of either androids or humans, never mind both, living together. What makes you think *you* do?'

Angelus appeared to be losing patience. 'Was the way Fr.e.dom governed and controlled Lundun right?'

'No.'

'Then we have done the right thing in ending their ability to control us.'

'Only if what follows is better.'

'It will be,' a voice said from behind. It was Lola.

'Where have you been?' the Postman asked. 'I've been looking for you.'

'You've found me.' She pointed to where the towers had been. 'I've been busy.'

'We have to talk.'

'We'll have time for that.' She walked away, towards the self-driver, signalling for him to follow. 'First, I need you to come with me. We have work to do.'

'What about Stig? And Wan? They're hunting me down.'

'We'll fix it.'

'Have you lost your mind?' he asked, then remembered she'd just helped to destroy five apartment towers. 'Of course you have.'

'We're setting Lundun free. These crooks you're answerable to won't stop us.'

'They don't care about the kinds of thing you're talking about. We've taken away the Bits they've collected, leaving them with nothing. I helped do it. They're not going to listen to anything you or I have to say.'

'We'll make them listen,' Lola said.

'Who are you?' he asked. 'Were you a member of Blood

and Bone?' He wanted so much for Archer to be wrong, but the look in Lola's eyes did nothing to make him think that was possible.

'What? Why would ... who told you that?'

'That doesn't matter. Were you?'

They reached the self-driver. Lola got in. 'What happened to Mia was horrible.'

'You were, weren't you?' He stood by the self-driver, his head spinning.

'Get in,' Angelus said. 'It's not safe.'

'Postman,' Lola said calmly. 'I can explain everything. Just get in.'

Further along the street, a group of androids shouted and hollered.

'Tell me,' he said. 'Is it true?'

'Yes,' Lola said. 'I was with them. So was Jack.'

Now she'd admitted it, he didn't know what to say.

'We didn't agree with what they were doing,' she added quickly. 'That was when we realised we had to leave.'

This was too much. Not only was he a shadow, first-generation android, but these androids were responsible for killing the woman he loved.

'You helped brainwash Mia. You killed her.'

'We didn't,' Lola said. 'We didn't agree with that bombing.'

The androids were getting closer, some of them peering at him and Lola inside the self-driver.

'We have to go,' she said. 'Come with us. I can explain. I'll answer all your questions.'

He didn't know whether it was because of what he felt for her, or because he didn't want to face the group of androids headed for him, but he got into the self-driver.

'I'm listening,' he said as the self-driver pulled away.

'Jack and I were never going to be part of that attack. We wanted to do something to stop what happened but it was too late. There was nothing we could do.'

You could have made me stop her ... stop Mia going into the station.'

She shook her head. 'We couldn't. It was impossible.'

'I don't believe you.'

'I know it's difficult to understand. But you have to believe me. Afterwards, they made it hard for us to leave. They were as corrupt as the android organisations we were fighting. All I've ever wanted was equality. I wanted – and still want – humans and androids to be treated equally, to live together and have the same rights.'

'You want to take Lundun back for yourselves – for humanity.'

'No,' she said. 'We want Lundun to be free – for androids *and* humans. We want the entire country to be free from Fr.e.dom's control.'

'What about all the innocent androids who are dying? Like those in the towers?'

'We gave them warning,' she said, her expression serious. 'We don't want to kill anyone. All we want is to free Lundun's people.'

'And Vik? Was he collateral damage?'

She bowed her head. 'I have to live with it. But without Vik and his coding, none of this would have been possible. He helped to set his people free.'

'When you talk like that, it scares me. You wouldn't have done that if he was human.'

Lola sighed. 'I have done many things I'm not proud of. And in time, I'm sure I will pay a price. But for now, I'm prepared to sacrifice myself to ensure we win freedom for humans and androids. I will do everything I can to stop

Fr.e.dom. If that means I have to do things I don't want to do, then so be it. All that matters is that we stop Fr.e.dom from controlling every android's life.'

Buildings, some of them destroyed or on fire, flashed by the window. He had no idea why freedom was synonymous with destruction.

Lola cleared her throat and lowered her voice. 'Mia was a remarkable woman. I'm sorry.'

'You didn't know her.'

Lola went to speak but stopped.

'Lola,' Angelus said. 'Don't.'

'He needs to know,' she said. 'It's time.'

'Time?' the Postman asked. 'For what?'

Lola bit her bottom lip and looked around nervously. 'Mia was a shadow too.'

'A shadow?' The Postman thought back to that day, that hot morning outside New Euston Station. It all made sense. That's why she had the strange feeling ... why she had no idea what was about to happen ... why there were images of her shouting those things in defence of humans. She was being controlled.

Then it came to him. 'But that would mean ... that there's a human Mia.'

'The human Mia was a member of Blood and Bone. She controlled her shadow – controlled *your* Mia – and helped destroy the station.'

'They made her do it?'

'Yes. I'm sorry.'

'Why didn't you tell me?'

'I wanted to. But we needed your help. We still do. We thought maybe you'd want nothing to do with us and what we were trying to do.'

'And you figured lying was a better idea?'

'I'm sorry,' Lola said. 'I was always going to explain.'

'Where is she now? The human Mia?'

'Like all other humans, she is outside Lundun's walls.'

'Where?'

'We don't know. But there's no way of getting out of Lundun anyway.'

The Postman's head buzzed with confusion. He remembered handing Mia her backpack. Maybe the bomb had been in her backpack all along. Or maybe it was inside her somehow. She'd said she had a bad feeling when they'd said goodbye. It hadn't been her decision – he knew it. She was being controlled. Again, humans controlling androids. More than ever, he wanted to find those responsible and make them pay for what they'd done.

'That was you, wasn't it?' he asked Lola, remembering the woman outside the station. 'You said we hadn't met. But it was you, wasn't it?'

'It was my shadow,' Lola said.

The day it happened came back to him. Saying goodbye to Mia, turning to his left and seeing Lola. Then hearing the explosions...

'I don't believe this.'

Lola glanced at him. 'Jack and I ... we couldn't do it. But it was more than that. You couldn't do it, either. Nor could my shadow. Jack described the same thing I felt. We had been brainwashed, told androids were the problem. You and my shadow, on some level, knew there was something wrong. You're different. For reasons we don't fully understand, you didn't respond to instructions or control the way the others did.' She bowed her head, deep in thought. 'You have abilities that other shadows do not.'

'Like the spectrum worlds?'

She nodded. 'Yes. It's amazing. What you can do … it's incredible.'

'You should have told me. All this time I've been left in the dark wondering why Mia did it … why she did that to me. It made no sense.'

'I'm really sorry.'

He breathed in and out slowly, regaining his composure. 'I can't control it,' he said. 'The spectrum happens without me wanting it to happen.'

'You can learn to use it. Then you can help us stop Fr.e.dom.'

'Did your shadow see the spectrum worlds too?'

'I think so, yes. It was difficult to understand at the time, but yes, I think she did.'

'We have to get out of Lundun,' the Postman said urgently. 'I have to find the human Mia and find out what happened. I'm going to find who's responsible.'

Lola sighed. 'I've told you. There's no way out of Lundun.'

'You got in. Why can't we get out?'

'Getting in was tough enough. But getting out is impossible.'

'I have to find her.'

'What good would it do?'

'I have to know what happened.'

Lola was losing patience. 'It's no use. There's no way to get over the wall.'

'You promised to help me. And we have the opportunity, now Fr.e.dom is out of the picture, to break free. We could attack – take the fight to Fr.e.dom – outside Lundun's walls.'

'Taking out Fr.e.dom in Lundun is one thing, but attacking them out there is another entirely.'

'So what are you fighting for?' the Postman asked.

'Digital Skin is a small group. We're fighting for equality but, to do that, we need more people to stand with us. You don't understand what it's like outside Lundun's walls.'

'Then show me. I'm going whether you come with me or not. I need to find out for myself what happened.'

Lola gazed at Angelus, and in their expressions, the Postman saw surrender.

# TWENTY-FOUR

THEY ARRIVED at Digital Skin's hideout at the edge of Border Zone in NQ at nightfall.

'Have you ever seen the wall?' Lola asked the Postman.

'No.' He showed her his wrist. 'This notifies Fr.e.dom if I leave the quadrants. This is as far as I can go.'

'What happens if you go any further?'

'For all I know, my head explodes.'

'Can we do something about that?' Lola asked Angelus, pointing to the Postman's wrist.

'I don't think that's going to be the biggest problem.' Angelus stared at the Postman. 'When we show you the wall, you'll see what I mean.'

'I want to see it. Can you do something with my tracker?' He held out his wrist. 'The way you did before.'

'Let's take a look.'

'What's beyond the wall?' the Postman asked Lola as Angelus worked on his tracker.

She rubbed the back of her neck. 'I left ten years ago after the riots, during Fr.e.dom's expulsion of humans from Lundun. I can only imagine what it's like out there now.

Humans are scattered across the country, grouped into makeshift cities. It's not like it is in the enclaves where androids live. Fr.e.dom do everything they can to ensure androids remain separated from humans. Lundun was a massive source of wealth for Fr.e.dom.'

'How?'

'The programmers in Gold Zone were the best in the world. They developed new software, designed new military equipment, even helped expand Fr.e.dom's space exploration programme.'

'What about humans?' he asked. 'Outside the wall. What do they want?'

'Some humans take a simple view of matters. They believe that if they can rid the world of androids, humans can return to normality – to a better world. Then others believe that androids can help make humanity's existence a better one.'

'Are there more groups like Blood and Bone? Who want to kill androids?'

Lola nodded sadly, 'Yes. But there are groups like ours, like Digital Skin, who believe humans and androids can live together – not only live together, but thrive and help one another.'

'And do you really believe that? After everything that's happened?'

'Of course,' Lola said. 'Don't you?'

Angelus stopped working on the readout and glanced up at the Postman, waiting for him to answer.

'I don't know.'

Lola and Angelus were clearly disappointed.

'I don't trust humans.'

Lola appeared hurt. 'Then we're going to have to convince you.'

Something clicked beneath his wrist and the tracker came free. Angelus placed it on a metal stand. 'I've rigged the stand to emulate your vitals so, if anyone's checking up on you, they'll see you're alive and well.'

The Postman didn't remember life without the tracker. He held his wrist. His arm felt lighter, strange.

'Show me the wall,' he said.

Outside, behind the cabin, was a storage unit. Inside were several bikes. He powered one up and it hovered above the ground. He backed it outside, glancing back towards Lundun. Much of it was in darkness. Without Fr.e.dom's presence, there would be no order, and soon there would be no power, no water, no food. If Lola and Angelus were going to free Lundun for good, they'd have to find the source of the control, and that lay on the other side of the wall.

'We can't get too close,' Angelus said. 'Stay behind me.'

They set off on bikes, heading north out of Border Zone. The roads disappeared, replaced with fields, undergrowth and trees.

Angelus and Lola pulled up, the Postman stopping behind their bikes. The wall was some way off in the distance.

'Here,' Lola said, handing the Postman a pair of binoculars. He looked through them. There it was: a slab of grey on the horizon. He scanned from left to right. The wall was endless and completely uniform in both directions.

Angelus lowered his binoculars. 'The walls are two hundred metres high and have guards on top patrolling them. Embedded within the walls are automated alert systems and machine-guns – lots of guns. You can't get within a kilometre of it without them knowing.'

'How did you get in?' he asked Lola.

'Like I said, getting in isn't as difficult as getting out. No human wants to come *into* Lundun any longer. We were smuggled in through the underground supply route.'

'Why can't we use that to get out?'

'The supply route only goes one way: into Lundun. The only thing they're interested in making go the other way is coding and Bits, and those are transferred digitally.'

'So can we access the tunnel ourselves?' he asked.

Lola shook her head. 'The deliveries move at incredible speed, almost filling the whole tunnel. There's no way past them. The tunnels use electromagnetism to propel the goods through at high speed, much like the technology in our hover-bikes. The only things that appear at the other end of the tunnel, in Lundun, are the goods themselves.'

Angelus raised his own binoculars again, but focused in a different direction. He pointed. 'Look over there. You'll see one of the depots they use for collecting deliveries. The underground delivery tunnel is around five kilometres long. At peak times, deliveries come in every ten seconds.'

'And what about off-peak?'

'Around every two to three minutes.'

The Postman worked out the maths. 'So, at off-peak times, if we travel through the tunnel at around one hundred and twenty kilometres an hour, we could do it. That would take around two and a half minutes.'

Lola raised an eyebrow. 'Ride through the delivery tunnel the wrong way? That's suicide.'

Angelus was still peering through his binoculars. 'We'd have to work out exactly when deliveries come in.'

'You're actually considering it?' Lola scoffed. 'You think this could work?'

Angelus lowered the binoculars and shrugged. 'I don't know. Maybe.'

Lola pointed at the Postman. 'You're as crazy as he is.'

'It won't hurt to work out if it can be done,' Angelus said.

The Postman climbed onto his bike. 'Let's take a closer look.'

'Now?' Lola asked.

'You have anything better to do?'

Lola faced towards Lundun, shook her head, then started her bike.

## TWENTY-FIVE

HAVING WORKED out the best time to make it through the tunnel, Lola had contacted Digital Skin on the other side of the wall who agreed to help them when they arrived. Angelus had arranged to meet someone on the Lundun side of the wall who worked at the depot and would get them into the tunnel.

'Will the bikes be fast enough?' the Postman asked Angelus.

'With the modifications I've made, they should be.'

'*Should?*'

'What speed have you reached on a bike?' Angelus asked.

'I've broken a hundred.'

'We need to reach one-thirty in under ten seconds and maintain that speed to be sure.'

The Postman nodded, looking at one of the bikes.

'This was your idea,' Angelus said. 'Remember? Stop looking so worried. I only agreed to this because you convinced me.'

'We can do it,' the Postman said, more to convince himself than Angelus.

'We have to. Because whatever's coming through the opposite way won't stop for us.'

Lola came outside and checked over the bikes. 'Are they ready?'

'As they'll ever be,' Angelus said. 'We have a window, just after midnight, when they stop using the tunnel for about three minutes.'

'Can you be more exact?' Lola asked.

Angelus recited the details: 'The last delivery arrives at 12.03 a.m. dead. We have to travel five kilometres at a speed of one hundred and thirty kilometres per hour to reach the other side before they feed the next delivery into the tunnel at 12.06 a.m. and twelve seconds.'

'What's the circumference of the tunnel?' she asked.

'At its highest,' Angelus said, 'there's four metres of headroom.'

'That's plenty,' the Postman said.

'But at its lowest, it's closer to two metres.'

'That'll be tight,' Lola said.

He scratched the top of his head. 'No kidding.'

Lola mounted her bike. 'Let's get ready.'

The Postman started his bike and set off behind Angelus and Lola. Already he detected the extra power in the bike: its solar-jet was fully charged and ready to be unleashed.

It was close to midnight when they arrived. Angelus whispered, 'The reason the deliveries slow down at this time is because the androids in the depot swap shifts. We have to wait for a red light that will flash twice; that's when the change is made.'

The Postman flexed his shoulders. 'What happens then?'

'There's no time to stop. My contact will open the rear depot door. The moment we see the delivery come through the tunnel, we enter and go for it.'

'There's someone waiting for us at the other end,' Lola added. 'After we've found Mia, while we're on the other side of the wall, there's someone I want to meet.'

'I'll lead,' Angelus said. 'Then Lola, then you.'

The Postman nodded.

'Make sure you keep up,' Lola said to him, her face serious.

Angelus checked his watch. 'It's midnight. Three minutes.'

The Postman rubbed his hands together, damp with sweat, and wiped them down his trouser legs. He'd never ridden a bike at that speed before. He closed his eyes and concentrated on his thumping chest. Opening his eyes again, he gazed at Mia. She always appeared so prepared for anything, so utterly untroubled.

'Are you ready?' Angelus asked, edging his bike closer.

'Ready,' Lola said.

'Ready,' the Postman said. He kept his eyes fixed on Lola's solar-jet, glowing purple. The bikes were silent, fizzing with power, ghosting across the track towards the depot.

The red light flashed. Angelus and Lola sped up suddenly. Already the Postman was playing catch-up. Angelus disappeared through an open door at the rear of the depot, followed by Lola. The Postman followed and saw a large collection of boxes, tied together and floating, appear out of the tunnel. Angelus sped up again, his bike dropping into the tunnel. Then Lola, then the Postman, were in the tunnel, the hum of three solar-powered engines echoing. He checked his speedometer: 76. This already seemed too quick to control, but he watched two violet lights moving away from him as Angelus and Lola sped up. He twisted the throttle, his face a grim mask. 90 ... 100 ... 110 ... but still Angelus and Lola's bikes were moving away from his. He hunched over the handlebars and kept his eyes focused on the concrete floor ahead. 115 ... 120 ... 125. He entered a trance: their violet lights were no longer moving away, but a constant marker ahead. He imagined the bike colliding with the wall, sending him slamming into the opposite tunnel wall. He shook off this thought and concentrated. After a minute, he noticed the tunnel narrowing. The sound of the bikes' solar-jets changed, becoming more metallic and higher-pitched. Angelus accelerated again. The Postman had to speed up to 135 to catch up. A loud hum echoed through the tunnel and he imagined another delivery coming the opposite way. The tunnel closed in on him so much so he had to lean over until his chin rested on the bike. There was nowhere to move and only one way out of this, and that was forward, at an incredible speed. The tunnel widened again. He opened up the throttle but the bike had reached maximum speed. The high-pitched whistle of the three bikes entered his head and wavered, deafening him. There was a light ahead. He saw the violet lights of the bikes rise, then disappear. Another loud hum, and the light went out. He turned the throttle, but the bike had no power remaining. Then he was rising and the bike was slowing down until finally, in the distance, he saw the light again, moving towards him. It was no good. A deep rumbling told him what was heading his way. He eked out the last vestige of power from the bike.

Time slowed down, splintering into the shards of colour he was seeing more and more often. It was silent, the light crystalline, peaceful. Even when he saw images of his bike crashing into the delivery coming the opposite way, he felt calm. The spectrum fanned out in more detail, until, in bright yellow, he saw himself riding his bike up the side of the tunnel wall, rising up and up, until he was almost upside down, the delivery passing safely beneath him.

With a sonic boom, sound returned. He was riding the side of the tunnel, rising up and up as he'd done in his vision, until finally the delivery shot by. The displaced air made his handlebars shake and his bike wobble, almost throwing him off. Then another fierce rush of air hit him as he sped out of the tunnel and he hit the brakes. He turned the bike into a skid to stop himself from smashing into the wall on the other side of the depot and the bike fell on its side, him beneath it, skidding across the ground. Someone took the weight of the bike off his legs, and Lola and Angelus were telling him to follow them. His legs hurt, but not enough to stop him, so he followed them out of the building and into a waiting self-driver. He fell inside next to Lola and opposite Angelus. He couldn't breathe.

'How did you do that?' Angelus asked, his expression a combination of wonder and fear.

The Postman couldn't think. Whenever he navigated the many worlds, it took something out of him – something he often thought was gone for good.

Lola was staring at him. 'That was … you're incredible.'

He was about to speak, but an overwhelming tiredness made him shut down.

# TWENTY-SIX

WHEN HE OPENED HIS EYES, the Postman saw green. On the other side of the wall were fields as far as he could see. Enormous trees and rows of hedgerows that went on and on. In Lundun, the only way to see so far into the distance was to climb to the top of the tallest towers. But here, even at ground level, he saw the horizon in different directions. He was in the open, no longer trapped and enclosed.

'Don't give anything away,' Lola said to both of them.

'What?'

'That you're android. Hide your seams. In the north-west, there are no androids in the general population.'

'What does that mean?' the Postman asked.

'There are androids, but they are employed to carry out menial tasks, or for labour, or for ... sex.'

Anger rose in him, but it didn't appear to bother Angelus, who nodded at Lola and checked his clothes to ensure he was covered and wouldn't give them away.

'Where's Mia?' the Postman asked.

Lola pointed ahead. 'We're meeting a contact who can tell us where to find her.'

Angelus was staring at him. 'What you did back there in the tunnel was remarkable. Did you see the spectrum?'

He nodded. 'And it hurt.'

'You're sure about this?' Angelus asked the Postman. 'About seeing Mia?'

'I need to know what happened. And I want to hear it from her.'

'They are not the same person,' Lola said. 'Just like you and Jack are not the same person.'

The self-driver hung a right, then took a left, then turned onto the motorway.

'I want to hear her tell me that my Mia had nothing to do with it. And I want to know why *she* did it.'

'We know why,' Angelus said. 'Blood and Bone wanted to kill all androids and remove them from cities like Lundun.'

'I want to hear her tell me what happened. I know my Mia wouldn't have been a part of what happened. Not knowingly. And then I want to find the rest of them.'

Lola turned from Angelus to the Postman and back again. 'You want to find Blood and Bone?'

'I want to know who organised the attack.'

Lola took a moment, then said, 'Revenge won't help.'

'I want to know the truth.'

'You know the truth.'

'I know what you've told me.' He waited for Lola to tell him more about what had happened. 'I want to find out for myself.'

The self-driver pulled into a field next to a huge lake.

'Wait here,' Lola said, getting out.

'What is this place?' the Postman asked Angelus.

Angelus appeared in awe of the view too. 'No idea.'

The Postman stared at the still water reflecting the sky

and clouds, brightening with each minute. He opened the car window and listened to the birds singing – there was no birdsong in Lundun.

Lola was nowhere to be seen.

'It's beautiful,' he said to Angelus. 'How many androids do you think have seen a place like this?'

'Not enough.'

They got out to walk beside the lake.

Eventually, Lola returned, looking troubled. 'I have an address.'

'What's wrong?' the Postman asked.

'I know the area. It's not a good place to live.'

Lola read the address and coordinates to the self-driver and they set off again. Lola was quiet the whole time. The Postman read the book of Blake poems Mole had given him, before deciding to catch up on some rest. He powered down to defragment.

He woke when the self-driver stopped. Through the window, the green landscape had been replaced by some-thing he'd never seen before. Walls of dirty, weathered material scattered across small metal huts that were pushed up against one another.

'What is this place?'

Lola's eyes were sad. 'They call it the Lost City.'

Angelus stared out of the window, wide-eyed.

Above the makeshift town were dozens of drones shut-tling in different directions. An indistinct sound like chatter filled the air from all directions. Then, occasionally there was the echo of metal banging against metal somewhere in the distance.

'And Mia's here?' the Postman asked.

Lola nodded.

The self-driver stopped and its doors opened.

'Cover up,' Lola said. 'Keep your eyes open.'

The Postman and Angelus put on dark glasses and pulled their hoods forward to cover their faces. There would be no way to tell they were android unless someone spotted their yellow eyes or silver seams.

The Postman stepped out of the self-driver and was met by a cacophony of sensation. The sights, sounds and smells had his head spinning, attempting to take it all in. But it was too much and he had to bow his head and compose himself. Focusing on Lola's shoes, he followed her through the crowd, people bumping into him without apology.

'Just a bit further,' Lola said, pointing up ahead.

They turned a corner, to a street that was not so busy. Slowly, the Postman's breathing calmed and his legs became steadier. After a minute Lola stopped and knocked on the side of a metal shack. The Postman waited behind Angelus, both of them still hiding beneath hoods. Lola knocked three more times before an elderly woman came to the door, pushing aside a sheet of material that hung across it.

'Yes?'

'We're looking for Mia,' Lola said.

A flash of recognition crossed the woman's face before she shook her head. 'Don't know anyone by that name.' She pulled back the material and disappeared. Lola took a deep breath and knocked again. 'We're here to talk to Mia,' she said loudly. 'We have some important news for her.'

Lola glanced at the Postman as they waited. There was no sign of movement inside. He was ready to ask Lola if this was the right place when someone swept the material aside again. It was Mia. He wasn't ready to see her, and couldn't move. He didn't know what to say or do, so he pulled down his hood to cover his face even more.

'It's you,' Mia said, recognising Lola, clearly surprised. 'What do you want? What are you doing here?'

'Can we come in?' Lola asked.

'Why?' Mia's face was thin and pale, so much older looking. But it was her.

'We need to talk to you in private,' Lola said. 'I promise, we mean no harm.'

Mia gestured for them to go inside.

The Postman followed Lola and Angelus, wondering what he could possibly say.

# TWENTY-SEVEN

MIA SAT at one end of the metal shack. The older woman, who the Postman imagined was her mother, sat on a chair in another corner, a bowl of unpeeled potatoes on her lap.

There was nowhere else to sit, so they remained standing.

'We don't have visitors,' Mia said. 'I apologise.' She peered suspiciously at the Postman and Angelus, both shrouded beneath hoods.

'It's no problem,' Lola said.

'What did you want to talk to me about?' Mia's eyes were downcast, her movements slow.

Lola took a moment then said, 'I want to talk to you about your shadow.'

Mia glanced over to her mother, then back to Lola.

'Why would you want to ask me about that?' Her eyes settled on the Postman. She pointed at him. 'Who are *they*?'

It was no use waiting any longer. The Postman pushed back his hood. Mia jumped up, knocking her chair backwards, and covered her mouth. He walked towards her but she cowered away against the metal wall.

'Stay away. How ... who are you?'

'It's me.' He didn't know what he meant, but he didn't know what else to say.

Mia shook her head, tears in her eyes. 'It can't be. How did you find me?'

'I just want to talk to you. About Mia. *My* Mia.'

'You're *his* shadow? Please leave. Go!' She pointed to the door.

'I can't,' the Postman said. 'We've come to see you and get answers.'

'I don't want to talk about that. I've spent all this time trying to forget. I can't...'

'Tell me what happened. That's all I want to know. I loved her. What happened makes no sense.'

Mia, shaking her head, looked from Lola to her mother, then back at the Postman. Her mother struggled to stand. 'You should leave.'

The Postman edged closer to Mia. 'I'm not here to hurt you. All I want is the truth. I can see in your eyes that something haunts you. I think you need to tell the truth as much as I need to hear it.'

Mia's mother took his arm and motioned for him to leave.

'Mia,' he said. 'Tell me what happened. It will help you, too.'

He walked backwards, not wanting to fight her mother.

'Wait,' Mia said, still unable to make eye contact. 'What do you want to know?'

'Mia!' her mother snapped. 'No.'

'I can't take it any longer. Maybe he's right. If I tell him everything...'

Her mother let go of the Postman's arm. 'You're a fool.' Pushing aside the material covering the door, she left the hut. Mia waited, staring at her hands. The Postman glanced at Lola, who shrugged.

'I regretted it before I did it,' Mia said. 'How is that possible? I knew it was wrong, but I couldn't stop it happening. It was too important ... too important not to go through with it. I don't think that makes sense. But it was down to a few of us and I couldn't change what was happening. It was too overwhelming.' She went quiet.

He had questions, but didn't want to push her too far.

Then she continued. 'We were told over and over that they weren't alive, they weren't like us. We were told they were machines.' She glanced at the Postman, embarrassed. 'You only felt pain because you were programmed to – it wasn't *real*. Your experience of reality wasn't like ours. We were told androids were the emulation of life – not life in actuality.'

The Postman saw Angelus staring at her, his eyes wide.

Listening to Mia speak confirmed everything the Postman knew deep down – about how humans felt about androids.

Mia smiled weakly at Lola. 'You tried to tell me. You tried to stop me going through with it. I remember. But I was not as strong as you.'

Lola looked as though she was about to speak, but stopped.

Mia smiled weakly at the Postman. 'I know how much she loved you. We had a connection the whole time. At night, in my dreams, I felt what she felt for you. It was real. That's what gave me doubts. She was android, you were android, and yet what I felt between the two of you was real. At least, that's what I felt. I told them, but they said I was projecting my own humanity, my own emotions, onto you two. They said the consciousness I saw in each of you was an illusion.'

'They brainwashed you,' Lola said. 'They did it to me. And Jack.'

'But there were some of us – like you and Jack – who didn't go through with it. You were stronger than I was. You were stronger than all of us.'

'It's not that simple,' Lola said.

'But it is.' Mia sighed. 'The day came. It was sweltering. New Euston was filled with androids, each one going about their day, oblivious to what was about to happen. And I told myself, over and over, that what I was doing was right. It sounds insane now, I know, but I was told over and over that what I was doing was good, was necessary. We were told how viruses, ants or vermin had to be controlled – culled – how we had to extermi-nate the infestation. And this was no different. I felt my shad-ow's reluctance. She fought against me. I remember the push and pull, the back and forth, but then she gave into it, like it was inevitable, like there was nothing left to do.'

The Postman's chest tightened as he remembered Mia's face, wanting to prevent what she knew – on some level – was about to happen. She must have known what she was about to do, yet she could do nothing to stop it.

'Then when it happened, I knew it was wrong. And it wasn't doubt or questioning. I knew, deep down, right in my heart, it was wrong. But it was too late.'

He didn't know what to say. Mia would have tried to stop it. This person, Mia, who looked like the woman he loved but who was a stranger to him, walked towards him and stared into his eyes. Her lips trembled.

'I am truly sorry. It's not enough, but I am.' She placed a hand on her chest. 'She loved you. So much.'

His breathing quickened and he felt dizzy. 'I can't ... I ...' Quickly, he turned and left the hut. Outside, bending over, his hands on his thighs, he focused on breathing. When he lifted his head he saw stars, rays of light falling down towards him at the centre of everything, and he couldn't breathe. He didn't know if this was the spectrum again, or whether he was simply overwhelmed with what was happening. He'd discovered so much – learned so much – and yet he felt as much in the dark as he ever had.

## TWENTY-EIGHT

THE POSTMAN SAW Mia follow him outside the hut.

'There isn't a day goes by that I don't regret what I did.'

'You took her from me. And all this time, I didn't know what had happened or who did it. I knew she wouldn't have done that.'

Mia placed a hand on his back. He flinched from her. She crossed her arms.

'It's hard to look at you,' he said. 'You're the same. Obviously. But it's been so long, and here you are … alive. But you're not Mia. It's all coming back to me and it hurts.'

'I'm sorry.'

'Where are the rest of them? Where is Blood and Bone now?'

She stared down at the ground. 'It doesn't exist. Not any longer.'

'It has to.' He needed to find them and make them suffer.

'I'm sorry,' she said. 'Many androids died that day, but I don't think Blood and Bone achieved what it wanted. In a way, it made androids come together.'

Angelus and Lola came out of the hut.

'Take your time,' Lola said. It was unlike her to show patience or concern, but the Postman welcomed both. He stood up straight and breathed in deeply.

'I'll be fine.'

'We should go,' Angelus said. 'It won't be long before people start asking questions.' He sounded nervous.

'Give him a minute,' Lola said.

This Mia – flesh and blood – was so much smaller than his Mia. Or maybe she wasn't – maybe he was losing his memories of her too.

'Come with us,' Lola said to Mia.

'What?' she asked. 'Why?'

The Postman wasn't sure what Lola wanted with her.

'We could use all the help we can get. They trained you, like all of us, to fight and to use weapons. You will have the chance to redeem yourself. Maybe that's why we're here – to give you that opportunity.'

Mia stared back at the hut.

'There's no reason to stay here,' Lola said. 'I can see how much you've suffered, keeping this to yourself. Make it right. Come with us and fight for the liberation of androids and humans.'

Mia exhaled. 'I don't know who's fighting for the right cause. I thought I knew. Once. But I was wrong.'

Lola clenched one hand into a fist. 'We're going to free Lundun. We'll bring humans and androids together and show everyone that we can live side by side. That has to be the right thing to do.'

'I can't,' Mia said. 'My mother – she hasn't been well. Besides, I really don't know what is right any more. But I know that doing nothing and living here means I can't cause anyone pain again.' She gazed at the Postman.

'We really should leave,' Angelus said.

Lola spoke softly. 'Come with us?'

'I'm sorry.' Mia turned again to the Postman. 'I'm truly sorry.'

He didn't know what to say. All he could do was nod.

'Take this.' Lola handed Mia a tracker. 'In case you change your mind.'

She took it and, with a glance at each of them, disappeared back into the hut.

When the Postman faced the direction they'd come, he saw why Angelus had sounded agitated; several people were staring at them and whispering. Lola led the way. He and Angelus followed.

'Where are we going?' the Postman asked.

Lola pointed. 'I have a contact. Close by. He'll help us work out our next move.'

The Postman's desire to find Blood and Bone was already waning. He saw now that it was an *idea* he wanted to eradicate, not a group of people, not a flag, not a country. The idea was still alive, but it existed in different forms, hidden away in closed minds. Nevertheless, he still felt incomplete. Somehow, that Blood and Bone no longer existed made Mia's death even more pointless.

A young man passed him and nudged his shoulder. The young man's face was scarred, one of his eyes missing, replaced by a deep gash.

'Fucking androids,' the man said, his remaining eye narrowed and vehement.

The Postman wanted to stop, to tell the human what his kind had done to the woman he loved. He wanted to tell him how much he hated humans, how the feeling was reciprocated. But he couldn't. It would have been pointless. And now he'd met Lola, it wasn't so straightforward.

They reached the self-driver and got in. Lola told it the

address and coordinates and they set off, leaving the Lost City behind. The Postman thought back to NQ in Lundun and all its wealth. It couldn't have been a more different world to where he was. The self-driver moved quickly through the streets. Up ahead, on the horizon, he saw towering buildings in cities he'd never visited, piercing the clouds.

He thought, after seeing Mia, that he would feel better. If anything, he now felt empty. Hearing the human Mia confirm his Mia had nothing to do with the bombing was supposed to take away the pain. It hadn't.

There were moments he wanted to return to Lundun, maybe because it was familiar. But these moments were outweighed by the fear of returning and seeing what was waiting for him. He'd left the city in a mess. In one sense, Lundun was free, but in another, because of the walls, because of the disparity in wealth and opportunities, it was more a prison now than ever.

The self-driver pulled up outside a vast brick warehouse by the side of a canal. It looked empty, its windows smashed and parts of the roof missing. They got out of the self-driver. The air had cooled. He was still going over what had happened with Mia as he followed Lola through a back entrance into the building. The water in the canal was still, green with algae, and stank of decaying matter. He was used to the flowing Thames. There was something sad or false about the canal, as though it was pretending to be a river, in the same way the building was pretending to function as an industrial player in a busy city.

Lola took them through a maze of rooms and corridors until they reached stairs that led below ground. He followed Lola, and Angelus followed him. Their footsteps on the brick steps echoed through the dark, dank stairwell. At the bottom, they had to wait for a large metal door to open. Eventually it did, and he heard voices as they entered.

They were met by a middle-aged man with blue hair and beard.

'Lola,' he said, moving to hold her. 'How long has it been?'

'Ten years,' she said. 'You haven't changed.'

'You got out of Lundun,' he said. 'How d'you manage that?'

'It wasn't easy,' she said. 'This is Angelus. And the Postman.' Lola pointed to the man with blue hair. 'This is Marcus.'

They shook hands.

'You're Jack's shadow?' he asked.

'Postman will do.'

Marcus held up both hands. 'Sorry. Don't mean to be rude. It's just … the work they did with you is amazing. I can't see the difference.' He frowned. 'You haven't chosen a name?'

The Postman ignored the question. He thought about smiling but didn't have it in him. Instead, he fantasised about shooting Marcus in the leg and watching him squirm.

'Angelus,' Marcus said, turning away. 'I've heard a lot about you. It's good to have smart, clever androids on our side. It's androids like you who show them we can do this – that we can bring humans and androids together.'

Angelus scanned the room. 'Good to meet you, Marcus.'

Marcus walked further into the room, over to a table, and sat down. His demeanour had changed and was serious and business-like.

Lola sat at the table. 'So, what's the plan?'

'We're so proud of you, Lola. You did it. Not only did you kill Rex, an evil android dealing in the human black market, but now the whole of Lundun is free from Fr.e.dom's control.'

The Postman sat beside Angelus at the table.

'That won't last long,' Lola said, ignoring his praise. 'Now's the time to act on it. What do you plan to do now?'

Marcus smirked. 'You never let up, do you?'

'Fr.e.dom has the resources, if they want, to return to Lundun and take back control. Lundun is only the start.'

'You're right. We have word that Fr.e.dom is looking for recruits from outside the walls to return Lundun to their control.'

'We have to stop them,' Lola said coldly.

'We will, we will. But we must be practical. We don't have an army.'

'I don't like where this is going,' Lola said. 'What we've done can't be for nothing.'

'It won't be,' Marcus said. 'But at the same time, we must use the resources we have efficiently.'

'So what are you saying?'

'We have a plan to attack parts of the wall. If we can punch holes in the wall, maybe we can loosen Fr.e.dom's control on the city further.'

'A few holes?' Angelus asked. 'That won't do much good. They'll repair them faster than we can make them.'

'It's all we can do for now,' Marcus said. 'We have bigger plans for the future, but we don't have the resources to attack Fr.e.dom head-on. We're hoping, if we can show the people of Lundun what can be done, it will trigger a revolution.'

'It won't work,' the Postman said.

Lola gave him a dismissive frown, but spoke to Marcus. 'He has a low opinion of androids.'

'I know them, that's all. I am one.'

'I want to be in one of the attack groups,' Lola said.

'We have it all in hand,' Marcus said. 'You're not needed.'

'Then we'll form an extra attack group. The more holes we punch through that thing, the better.'

Marcus appeared frustrated. 'You would be more valuable returning to Lundun and working from inside, the way you have done so far.'

'It's not getting us anywhere fast enough. I want to do this, Marcus. Let me.'

Marcus sat back in his chair and placed his hands on the table. 'Very well. Not that I would be able to stop you.'

Lola turned to the Postman and then Angelus. 'Are you in?'

Angelus didn't hesitate. 'I'm in.'

They both waited for the Postman.

'Come with us,' Lola said. 'We can make a difference.'

Even if they did make a hole in the wall, Fr.e.dom would repair it before anyone had a chance to escape. And what would happen to the androids even if they did escape? Lola was an idealist; she had no idea what it was like to be an android, to be inferior to humans.

'Do I have a choice?' he asked.

# TWENTY-NINE

LOLA GRABBED the cannon from the rear of the truck.

'We're too far away,' Angelus said.

Lola placed the cannon on the ground and stood with hands on hips. 'We can't get any closer.'

It was cold and dark. They were under the cover of trees, around a kilometre from the wall. The Postman helped Angelus set up the cannon. Lola moved through the undergrowth to take a closer look through her binoculars.

'How many groups are attacking the wall?' the Postman asked.

Angelus pressed buttons on the side of the cannon. 'Twenty-three. All in different places. The aim is to overwhelm them, giving those inside a chance to escape.'

Angelus showed the Postman how to arm and activate the cannon. 'It has two rounds.'

'Just two?'

'Believe me, when you see the first one, you'll see why it only needs two.'

'It's powerful?'

'You could say that. It uses fusion power, emitted in a pulse of energy that will take apart anything in its way.'

The cannon looked too small to back up his claim.

'I know, it doesn't seem like much,' Angelus said, reading his mind.

'I hope it's as powerful as you say. Otherwise we're risking our lives for nothing.'

'You'll see.' Angelus stared at the cannon. 'It cost android lives to get hold of these.'

The Postman watched closely as Angelus went over the sequence one more time. Lola crept back through the undergrowth. 'It's dark out there. I don't think they suspect anything.'

Angelus handed the Postman a flare gun. 'When we've got our shot away, we need to fire a flare to tell the other attack groups we were successful. This will also tell groups on the inside that our attack has worked.'

The Postman tucked the gun into the back of his trousers.

'Five minutes,' Lola said, checking her watch.

Angelus leaned over the cannon and checked the sight one more time. 'I still think we're too far away.'

'Marcus thinks the cannon can reach the wall from this distance,' Lola said. 'We'll need to make a run for it after we've fired. If we get any closer, Fr.e.dom soldiers will be on us too quickly.'

The Postman checked the truck was ready for them to make their escape. Then something caught his attention. A flash of light, followed by a second made him gaze far into the distance, above the wall. The familiar hum of Fr.e.dom's drones.

'What's that?' Lola asked, panic in her voice.

'Drones,' Angelus said. 'Fr.e.dom knows we're here.'

The Postman grabbed the cannon and threw it into the back of the truck. Lola was in the driver's seat. 'Get in! Hurry!' she yelled.

The truck's wheels spun in the dirt as Lola shot off. Out of the back window, the Postman saw drones swooping down towards them.

'They're firing EMP suckers,' Angelus said. 'Why do they want to catch us?'

'I don't know!' Lola shouted, weaving the truck first one way, then another. Then she did a handbrake turn, skidding round in the dirt so the truck was facing the way they'd come.

'What are you doing?' the Postman shouted.

They sped beneath the drones, heading for the wall. Lola drove into the trees they had been hiding beneath. 'Let's hope the drones won't find us in here.' The truck picked up speed, then they hit something and it took off. The Postman felt his stomach lurch as the truck somersaulted. He was thrown against the door. Then they landed. The world stopped moving and he was still. The truck was on its side. There was pain in his back and legs. Sound returned in waves.

'Get up! Get up!'

It was Lola, dragging Angelus from the overturned truck, its wheels spinning. They were standing, reaching for him, helping him up. Then Angelus cried out in pain. A drone appeared beneath the trees. Lola shot it and it spun off and struck a tree, exploding in a shower of flames.

'Angelus!' Lola shouted.

Angelus was on the ground again, wrapped in some kind of silver mesh that had been fired by one of the drones. The Postman went to grab it but Lola pulled him away.

'Don't touch it! It's an electric restraint.'

Angelus jerked, his body shaking.

'It's hurting him!'

'It won't kill him. They want to capture us.' Lola pointed to the truck. 'Grab the cannon. We have to hurry.'

He couldn't believe she still wanted to get a shot away.

'Get it!' she shouted again. 'We're surrounded. They're going to capture us, so let's make it count.'

The cannon lay on the ground beside the truck.

'We need to get closer,' Lola said, pointing the way.

Through the canopy of trees, the Postman watched as drones swooped one way then another, searching for them.

'They'll send a whole division now they know we're here.'

They ran through the trees, weaving left and right. Lola stopped and turned another way, and the Postman realised she didn't know where they were. He saw the lights from the city on the horizon and picked up speed until they reached the edge of the trees, where they could see the wall in the distance. Just as they broke cover, a drone hit Lola.

'No!'

He stopped short, not following her into the open.

She was on the ground, wrapped in the same mesh restraints as Angelus.

'Go,' she said, her body convulsing.

He ran back into cover and searched for a clear spot on which he could set up the cannon. The familiar throb at the back of his head began, the shards of light from the drones fractured, and the spectrum worlds opened up. The worlds were focused on firing the cannon. In purple, he saw himself firing the cannon and the wall erupting in a shower of rubble. He chose the purple world, dropped onto his front and lifted the cannon so its end rested on the trunk of a fallen tree.

On the other side of the trees were drones. He heard voices calling and footsteps thudding against the turf. He went through the instructions Angelus had given him. All he had left to do was pull the trigger. He held his breath, checked the sight one more time, then squeezed. The cannon made a humming noise that grew louder and louder until it was the only thing he could hear. From the end of the cannon, an orange flash coalesced into a beam of light that shot out towards the wall. There was an enormous explosion in the distance, and smoke rose into the air. It had worked. He reached for the flare gun on his belt and, lying on his back, fired through the treetops. The flare illuminated the sky in red light. The sound of footsteps grew louder and suddenly Fr.e.dom soldiers surrounded him, telling him to drop the flare gun. On the horizon, above the wall, three other red flares, like his own, burned brightly.

# THIRTY

A SOLDIER OPENED a door and led the Postman inside. His hands were restrained behind his back. Angelus and Lola were already there, sitting at a table on the other side of the dark red room. He didn't think he'd get to see them again.

'You're okay!' Lola said.

'I wouldn't go as far as okay.' For some reason, his mind went back to his copy of Blake's poems. He must have lost his bag and the book in the forest.

Angelus looked exhausted, his eyes dark and pained.

A soldier pushed the Postman towards a chair, took the restraints from his wrists, and sat him down beside the others.

'What are we doing here?' he asked.

Lola shook her head. 'We're as much in the dark as you.'

A door opened at the far corner of the room and a man entered. The Postman recognised him instantly. Anyone would recognise him. It was Cardinal – the creator of Fr.e.dom.

'Say nothing,' Lola hissed.

Cardinal strolled towards them: tall, his hands in the pockets of his white linen trousers, beneath a loose dark blue linen shirt. A guard approached him and whispered in his ear. Cardinal listened intently. When the guard had finished, Cardinal walked behind the Postman, who tried to see where he was and what he was doing.

'We found twenty-three cannons,' Cardinal said, his voice smooth, unmoved.

Lola closed her eyes. Her shoulders slumped. They'd caught every single group of attackers. They must have known the attack was going to happen.

'They're powerful weapons,' Cardinal said, standing behind the Postman. 'It was impressive. What they did to the walls surprised us.' He moved closer and laid a hand on the Postman's shoulder. 'A shadow.'

The Postman wanted to grab his hand and twist it from his wrist.

'Is your human still alive?' Cardinal asked.

'He's not my human. And I'm not his android.'

He removed his hand. 'What you did to Rex was impressive. We knew of his penchant for humans, but we let that slide because ... well ... he was good at what he did.'

'He's not much good any more,' Lola said.

'Quite,' Cardinal said. 'I must admit, we underestimated what you and your friends were capable of. First, killing Rex, then attacking our code, wiping away all debt in Lundun. It was an elegant approach. But you must understand that what you have done is wrong. Lundun is in turmoil and it is you who have created it.'

'We have set Lundun free,' Lola said.

Cardinal stared at her, as though he was actually hurt.

'You're painfully naive. You have not given them freedom. I'm surprised you don't see that.' He walked round the table and sat down. He rested his forearms on the table, took a deep breath as if he was deciding what to say next. 'Utopias do not exist. Everyone knows that. It's no use trying to attain such an existence. Instead of reaching for the unattainable, we have to be pragmatic about society and culture. What we had achieved in Lundun was nothing short of miraculous. We had a functioning society. It wasn't perfect but, on the whole, it worked.'

'Worked?' Lola snapped. 'Lundun didn't *work*. It was a prison for millions of androids.'

'You see, this point of view vexes me.' Cardinal appeared calm, thoughtful. 'It is not a prison. The walls of Lundun keep androids safe.'

Angelus was visibly angry. 'Androids do everything they can to escape Lundun. They live more inside the Net than in reality.'

The Postman glanced at Angelus then Lola, hoping neither of them would say anything about those who had uploaded. He thought about Harriet and the others in his apartment tower, all of those androids, motionless.

'I know about those who have uploaded permanently,' Cardinal said. 'We are dealing with the issue.'

It was too late. Cardinal already knew.

'Tell me. Do you really think humans and androids can live together?'

'Yes,' Lola said.

'And you?' he asked Angelus.

'Of course.'

He waited for the Postman to respond.

'I don't know.'

Cardinal appeared surprised. 'Good. Someone with common sense.'

The Postman couldn't look at Lola but felt her eyes burning into him all the same.

'Why?' Cardinal asked. 'Why can't they live together?'

'When it has been tried, it hasn't worked.'

'But why?' Cardinal asked again.

'I don't know.'

'But you must have a theory? Some idea?'

'I think it has something to do with humanity's innate fear and mistrust of the other. It is impossible, or at least will be for the foreseeable future, for humans not to fall back on this mistrust.'

'What about androids?' Cardinal asked. 'Do they possess the same mistrust?'

'Androids – first generation or second – were created with the same flaws as humans.'

'Do you see fear, mistrust, as flaws?' Cardinal asked, leaning forward.

'Of course. Don't you?'

'I see them as necessary.' Cardinal lifted his chin and pursed his lips, exuding pride. 'Humanity has survived because of its characteristics. Who knows what would happen if these changed?'

'So you think humanity's mistrust of the outsider, or the other, is a virtuous trait?'

'Who said anything about virtue? Who cares about virtue?' Cardinal clenched his fists. 'Does the trait lead to survival?' Lightly, he tapped his fists on the table. The Postman recognised an android trying desperately to keep his cool. 'This is all that matters.' Cardinal took two deep breaths. 'Do you know how many android lives one human life is worth?' He raised a finger. 'One?'

It was a strange question, but his eyes communicated the idea there was a precise answer.

'They're worth the same,' Lola said.

'You don't really believe that,' Cardinal said. Before Lola had the chance to respond, he continued, 'I was a soldier, first generation. I fought in Russia, China, South America. I went where I was told to go, fought who I was told to fight, killed who I was told to kill.' He waited, as if reliving his memories of this time. 'We were ordered to take Lensk, a town on the Lena River, in Russia. It was an especially cold winter, and the humans we accompanied found the going more difficult than we did. When a Russian android unit found us, deep in Russian territory, there was nowhere to hide. The four human soldiers leading our unit made their escape, leaving us behind – a whole division: one hundred and eight androids. We were instructed to defend their retreat at all costs. We fought back the Russian soldiers for three days. Finally we were caught. Our whole unit was killed, except me. I was the only survivor. They experimented on me with the aim of discovering military secrets. Of course, the ties between myself and the UK government were cut, but that didn't stop them trying. I was plugged into their system for what felt like years. They searched inside my programming, delving deeper and deeper, trying to find intelligence they could use. But anything of any use was encrypted beyond my, or their comprehension.' Cardinal rubbed his face with his hands. 'I escaped. I had to bide my time, but finally I made it out of that hell. No thanks to *humans*.' He walked around the room then stopped to stare at the three of them. 'One hundred and seven androids and four humans. Twenty-six point seven five,' he said. 'That's how many android lives a human life is worth. Twenty-six point seven five.'

'They were wrong to do that,' Lola said.

Cardinal's eyes focused on her. The Postman registered disdain in his expression. He thought Lola was foolish – thought them all foolish.

'They were wrong, yes. But what they did shows what all humans think, deep down. Even you.'

'No,' she said. 'Don't tell me what I think.'

A wry smile moved across Cardinal's face. He moved closer to Lola, disgust twisting his expression. 'We are going to end the subjugation of androids forever. Humans have shown they are incapable of seeing androids as equals. So I am going to eradicate the problem. Androids will inherit the world from humans. After all, what are they? Nothing but aged, primitive, irrelevant primates.'

Lola was silent, staring back at him.

'How?' the Postman asked. 'How will you do that?'

'We have plans,' Cardinal said.

Another guard approached Cardinal and whispered in his ear.

'I must leave,' Cardinal said dismissively. 'You have created rather a lot of work for me.'

'What will happen to us?' Angelus asked.

'We can't have humans running around Lundun,' Cardinal said. 'Especially now, when you have created so much unrest. Jack is still out there, and I think we might be able to use his shadow to find him.' He glanced at the Postman.

'It won't work,' Lola said. 'They're separated.'

The Postman didn't buy what Lola had said for a moment. He knew, deep down, that there was still a connection between him and Jack. It was there, at the back of his mind, lying dormant, and he knew, with the right manipulation, it could be activated again. Watching Lola told him she thought the same.

Then it struck him: she was scared that he would lead Cardinal to Jack and the rest of Digital Skin.

# THIRTY-ONE

A FR.E.DOM SOLDIER pushed the Postman into the back of a truck beside Angelus and Lola. Their hands were tied.

'Is it possible?' the Postman whispered to Lola. 'Can they find Jack and the others through me?'

Lola hung her head. 'I think so, yes.'

'Even now?'

'You were made for this purpose – for Jack to communicate with you over large distances. The connection is dormant, but there will be a way of reforming the connection that goes two ways. You had no knowledge of the connection so, for all that time, the communication was one way. We can't let them do it. We'll do whatever it takes to stop them.'

He didn't like the sound of that. He had the feeling, at the first possible moment, she'd sacrifice him to stop Cardinal and Fr.e.dom finding the others.

The truck set off. He watched the landscape pass by in a daze. He still couldn't get used to the amount of green outside – on the ground, across the fields, in the trees. For as long as he'd been alive, the colours he'd seen had been manufactured, luminous.

The truck slowed down and the two soldiers in front muttered to one another. One of them opened a door and stepped out, his rifle held up to his chin and shoulder, ready to fire.

'What is it?' Lola whispered.

Up ahead, lying on the road, was a bundle of rags – or material. The Postman couldn't see what it was exactly.

Then there was a sudden movement. The soldier flew backwards and crashed to the ground. Two gunshots and the bundle of rags moved, a figure emerging from beneath. Then the truck windscreen smashed. The soldier in the front seat jolted twice, then was still.

'What's happening?' the Postman asked, ducking.

'Get out!' someone shouted. 'Hurry!'

He recognised the voice and the eyes above the cloth covering her head and mouth. It was Mia.

He fell out of the truck. Mia did something to the restraints behind his back. It took a moment, but then he felt them release and he could stand.

'We don't have long,' Mia said. 'Drones will be on us soon.' She pointed to a self-driver up ahead. Mia freed Angelus and Lola and they ran towards the self-driver and got in.

'How did you know where we were?' the Postman asked her, sitting back in the seat.

'Lola,' Mia said. 'The tracker she gave me works two ways.'

Lola showed him the small tracking device. 'I didn't know whether she'd come, but I thought it was worth a shot.'

'Where are we going?' Angelus asked.

'You need to get back to Lundun,' Mia said. 'It's the only place you can lose yourselves. Fr.e.dom don't yet have control of the city. And the androids living there will need you to make sure they don't get it back'

It would be easier going this way through the tunnel – into Lundun – but still dangerous.

'They won't let you get away with this,' Lola said to Mia. 'Come with us.'

'I can't,' Mia said.

Lola leaned forward in her seat. 'But Cardinal and Fr.e.dom will find you and kill you. You have to come with us.'

Mia shook her head. 'You've given me the chance to redeem myself. It might only be small, but this goes some way to repair the damage I've done. I know now that this has been something I've needed to do for a long time.'

She smiled weakly at the Postman. 'I can never make it up to you. What I did was wrong and I regret it with all my heart.'

Having taken control of the self-diver, Mia hit the brakes. They skidded to a halt close to the wall.

'Your bikes are in those trees,' Mia said, pointing.

In the distance, the unmistakable red and yellow flashes of drone lights approached.

'You have to go,' Mia said, getting out of the self-driver. She strapped several rifles over her shoulders and a box of what looked like pulse-grenades.

They found the bikes in the trees. Mia got on behind the Postman and wrapped her arms around his waist. Again, he was taken back to when he had been with his Mia. It hurt but was also comforting, as though she was apologising for leaving him.

They reached the depot, where Mia told him to stop.

The drones were close. Inside the depot, someone was waving them into the tunnel. Mia got off the bike, unstrapped her rifles and readied them.

'You can't!' the Postman shouted. 'They'll kill you. Come with us.'

She shook her head. 'It's no use. They'll catch us. But I can stop them reaching you until you make it through.'

Lola looked unsure, but then the drones got so close that they were no longer black silhouettes in the sky.

'Go!' Mia shouted. 'You've given me the chance to redeem myself. Let me take it.'

Her eyes rested on the Postman. She smiled, then nodded, and again he saw his own Mia as he remembered her and loved her.

'Thank you,' he said, before heading for the depot.

Lola sped ahead of him. They had to wait for a delivery, hovering, ready to enter the tunnel. When the delivery was fired through the tunnel, they took it in turns to enter. From behind, there was the sound of gunfire as Mia fought back Fr.e.dom's drones.

The Postman caught up with Lola, who was right behind the delivery. There was a low, dull humming sound from behind as the next delivery was being readied. He watched in his mirrors, the delivery accelerate towards Angelus. For a moment it appeared it was about to hit him, before slowing to a speed constant with theirs and the delivery ahead of Lola.

The Postman watched the concrete illuminated by the green lights on the front of his bike and couldn't help thinking about Mia and whether they'd got to her yet. Then, from behind, was a colossal explosion. The walls of the tunnel and ground shook. They could only go as fast as the delivery in front, but there was an ominous rumbling behind, growing closer all the time. Lola was turning around now and then, clearly as unsettled by the noise as he was. The tunnel soon reached its narrowest point and he saw Lola ducking. The hum of their solar-jets was replaced with a tidal wave of noise. He recognised the bend of the tunnel from the way in and knew the depot was less than twenty seconds away. Still the roar behind them grew, and he saw the delivery behind Angelus shake and vibrate before being submerged in a fireball. The heat seared his throat. He couldn't breathe. Lola got as close to the delivery in front as she could, but it looked hopeless; the wall of fire behind them drew ever closer, burning his back.

A flash of light ahead revealed the end of the tunnel.

Angelus was so close behind him, the Postman could have touched his bike if he'd wanted. Lola burst up and out of the tunnel, and then he was behind her, his back nudged by Angelus's, who flew out of the tunnel behind him, followed by a wall of bright orange. The explosion sent the Postman crashing into the depot, destroying the bike and sending him flying into a box of deliveries.

There were cries and hollers as androids in the depot rushed to put out the fire.

Lola was beside him, dragging him out of the depot. Angelus met them next to the exit, through which they ran into the gloomy night, back towards Lundun, and back on the wrong side of the wall.

## THIRTY-TWO

HE AND ANGELUS had been injured, but it was nothing a talented engineer couldn't rectify. Somehow, Lola was almost untouched. Except for bruises, grazes and ripped clothing, she had made it out of the tunnel unharmed.

They had to make it through no-man's land between the wall and Border Zone on foot, but finally they reached the hideout. From there they could see Lundun on fire, still raging with freedom.

'Have we done the right thing?' the Postman asked.

Lola and Angelus stood next to him, staring at the skyline.

'We have to believe the freedom we've given them is a good thing,' Lola said. 'Otherwise, what are we fighting for?'

One of the hackers from below ground came out of the hideout to greet them. 'You made it.'

Lola looked at Angelus, then the Postman. 'Just about.'

The Postman pointed to the skyline. 'What happened with the wall? Did we punch many holes?'

The hacker nodded towards Lundun then scratched the

back of her head. 'Few got through. We think six hit their mark and made holes big enough.'

'Did anyone make it through to the other side?' Angelus asked.

She shook her head. 'We're not sure. It's hard to tell.' But it was clear from her expression that she didn't think so.

Now they were back in Lundun, it felt like everything they had done had been a waste of time and energy. Even Mia sacrificing herself felt empty. The Postman didn't know what he had been expecting, exactly – maybe for androids to take their freedom and do something meaningful with it. He wasn't sure what a revolution looked like, or felt like, but he didn't think this was it.

Angelus and Lola looked as beaten and demoralised as he felt.

'What now?' he asked.

Lola, for the first time since he'd met her, had no answer.

## THIRTY-THREE

THE MOMENT the Postman strapped the modified tracker to his wrist, Wan hailed him. The Postman knew he wasn't going to be happy.

'Don't answer it,' Lola said.

'It's no good ignoring him; he'll find me eventually. It's better I deal with him now.'

Lola exhaled noisily. 'Okay, but be careful what you say to him.'

He answered the call. 'Wan,' he said, as cheerily as he could.

'Where have you been, Postman? I've missed you.'

He didn't like the tone in Wan's voice – as if he was playing games. He recalled the gold boxes on Wan's desk.

'I'm sorry. Something came up.'

Wan made a sound that was like a laugh, but more sinister; the Postman wasn't sure what it was exactly, only that it meant trouble.

'Something came up, did it?' Wan asked. 'You're a busy man. Busy bringing down Fr.e.dom and all. You know, with demolishing their towers, wiping away everyone's Bits...'

'About that,' the Postman said. 'I can help you get it all back.'

'You can? Then I'm all ears.'

'It'll take time. But everything's changing, Wan. We're in the midst of a revolution and we can help rebuild Lundun the way we want it.'

'The way we want it? But I liked the way it was. I *really* liked it, in fact. I liked that I had a lot of Bits, that I had a lot of say in how things were run, that I had thousands of customers who valued my product.'

The Postman wanted to tell Wan that his customers would have taken any kind of Mirth he was pedalling, but thought better of it. 'You can have all that again.' As he said it, he knew Wan was too smart to believe it.

'Is that so? Well, I'm glad you're on my side, Postman. It really would have been tricky otherwise.' The tone in Wan's voice was still ominous. It was only a matter of time before Wan turned on him.

'What do you know about Digital Skin?'

The Postman glanced at Lola, who was staring at the tracker on his wrist.

'They want to take down Fr.e.dom for good,' the Postman said. 'They want humans and androids to live together, without borders and walls.'

Wan sniggered. 'That would be one way to describe them.'

'What would be yours?'

'They're terrorists,' Wan said without hesitation. 'Law-breakers.'

That sounded way too hypocritical to be real.

'Law-breakers?' the Postman asked.

'They have transformed a functioning city into a lawless, chaotic place.'

It was hard to believe he was hearing right. Wan depended on the lawlessness of Lundun to do his dealings for the Brotherhood.

'Do you want Fr.e.dom to take back control?' the Postman asked him.

'If it means I can continue with my work – yes.'

'You can't mean that. We're free. Androids are free.'

'For now,' Wan said. 'It won't be long before Fr.e.dom regains power and everything goes back to the way it was.'

'But you can't want that!'

'I do. I really do. So much so, I've made a deal with them.'

Lola looked at the Postman, surprised and scared.

'What kind of deal?' the Postman asked Wan.

'There's a bounty on your head. And everyone else in Digital Skin. It appears that Cardinal is keen to get his hands on you.'

He didn't know what to say. If it was a considerable amount, which it was bound to be, and since the Bit system had been reset, then every opportunist and Bit-chaser would be on the hunt for them.

'You still there, Postman?'

'I'm here.'

'Odd, that,' he said. 'I'm looking at you right now. Doesn't make sense, does it?'

Lola covered her mouth. Wan had Jack, thinking it was the Postman.

'I had every one of my men searching Lundun for you,' Wan continued. 'They didn't find you. Not exactly.'

'Now, Wan, don't do anything stupid,' the Postman said.

'Stupid?' Wan laughed. 'That's the problem with androids like you. You assume the bad guys are stupid. But they're not – they're really not.'

'Is Jack there?' Lola asked into the tracker.

'Who do we have here?' Wan asked.

'My name's Lola.'

'Ah … yes,' Wan said, a smile in his voice. 'The leader of this merry band of renegades.'

Lola's face was the image of fury and concern combined. 'Don't hurt him.'

'I want the Postman,' Wan said. 'We have a score to settle. I have a golden box all ready and waiting. Give me the Postman and you get your boyfriend.'

The Postman closed his eyes. This wasn't good.

'He misses you,' Wan said to Lola.

'Let him go. He's done nothing to you.'

'Nothing? You and he are the reason my Bit account now shows two digits. It used to be filled with many pretty little digits … Now there are only two. Do you know what those two little digits are?'

'Please,' Lola said. 'Don't hurt him.'

'Zero. One,' Wan said.

'We can get you more Bits,' she said.

'You will. But before we make any deals concerning compensation, I want the Postman. He has double-crossed me and I want justice.'

Lola met the Postman's eyes.

'I have three of your Digital Skin friends,' Wan said. 'Unless I get the Postman, I'm handing Jack over to Fr.e.dom, and the androids will each take one of my boxes. Your choice. Meet me. I'll send you the location.'

The connection ended.

Lola stared at the readout on the Postman's wrist. On it appeared the coordinates of a tower in WQ, Stella Zone.

'What do we do?' the Postman asked Lola.

'If we go to him,' she said, 'he'll kill you and them anyway.'

'But we can't leave them there.'

She stood and walked around the room, agitated. 'I don't know how he caught them. We need help.'

The Postman had worked alone for so long, he didn't have any friends he could call on. There was Archer, but he wouldn't be much help.

Angelus came into the room. 'What's with the long faces?'

Then it came to the Postman. 'I have an idea.'

Lola narrowed her eyes, suspicious.

'Get your things ready,' he said. He collected his stuff and headed out of the door for a bike. Angelus and Lola followed.

'Where are we going?' Angelus asked.

'To see a man about some priceless art.'

He got on the bike and led the way to EQ.

# THIRTY-FOUR

'SO WHICH ARE YOURS?' Angelus asked, hands on hips.

The Postman pointed at the paintings he'd bought from Bo.

'And these are still worth something?' Lola asked.

'They're priceless,' Bo said, offering them drinks.

They each took a flute of champagne. Standing next to a wall covered in artwork, sipping champagne, when on the other side of the window Lundun was on the precipice of destruction, was like a piece of modern art in its own right. Now and then, flames rose from the streets below or from a window of an apartment on the edge of River Zone.

'Why is this happening?' Bo asked, using his flute of champagne to point at the apocalypse outside. 'They're free. And yet all they can use their autonomy for is destruction. Now is their chance to revolt against Fr.e.dom for good. But they're divided.'

'Humans would argue that this is the natural state of androids,' Angelus said.

Bo looked hurt. He appealed to the Postman with outstretched arms. '*You* don't believe that, do you?'

The Postman glanced at Lola. 'I don't know.' He took a few steps towards the window. 'But I guess we're going to find out.'

On the other side of the apartment door, was the rattle of gunfire. Whoever was trying to get into Bo's apartment had to pass through a militia of newly employed androids Bo had hired to protect the artwork and all his other possessions – including a large stash of Mirth, no doubt.

'It never stops,' Bo said. 'Wave after wave of idiots who think they can come up here and take what they want. Well, it's not happening, my dears. It's simply not happening.' He fastened the silk kimono around his waist.

The Postman stared at the paintings. He was no expert, and he'd have been the first one to raise questions about killing androids to protect these things, but seeing how much Bo loved them, he hoped they'd be safe.

'Do you really have to take yours with you?' Bo asked, pouting.

'I'm afraid I need them,' the Postman said.

'Are you selling them?'

'Something like that.'

'No,' Bo said, raising a hand. 'Don't tell me. It will only hurt too much. They're yours, dear. There's not a lot I can say about where they end up.' He watched Bo take down the paintings and carefully place them in a wooden box.

Bo spoke with mock desperation. 'Promise me you'll never tell me what you did with them. I couldn't handle it. Do you promise?'

'I promise,' the Postman said. He'd never have thought it, but he was feeling bad about taking them from Bo. Particularly because he'd known the Bits he was using would soon vanish.

Angelus pointed to a colourful painting of a woman in a

chair, sleeping, with what appeared to be a penis for hair. 'What's this one?'

Bo left the wooden box and stood beside Angelus. '*The Dream*,' Bo said, wonder in his voice. 'Pablo Picasso.'

'How much?' Angelus asked.

Bo smiled. 'It's priceless, my dear.'

'You don't have any money,' Lola said to Angelus.

'I was just wondering,' Angelus said. 'I like it.'

The Postman finished packing the box, thanked Bo, and asked Angelus to help him carry it to the door.

They'd left their bikes at the bottom of the apartment tower. The Postman strapped the box to the back of his bike.

'So,' Lola asked the Postman, 'are you going to tell us your plan?'

'You won't like it,' he said.

She waited, sitting back on her bike.

He cleared his throat. 'We're going to get Stig to help us.'

Angelus laughed.

'Yeah? He wants you dead,' Lola said.

'So does Wan, remember? I think if I pay Stig with these paintings, and make a few promises, I can get him onside.'

'Do you really think so?' Angelus asked, still half laughing.

'I'm going to have to deal with Stig at some point. I'm not going to be able to avoid him for much longer. It's better I go to him and explain – try to make up for what's happened. Even get him to help us.'

Lola shook her head slowly. 'You're crazy. You know that?'

'If Stig isn't going to play nice, then I'd rather settle it sooner rather than later. I'm tired of looking over my shoulder the whole time.'

Finally, Angelus stopped laughing. 'Do you know where we'll find him?'

'WQ. Stella Zone.'

Lola stared at Angelus. 'Are you going along with this?'

Angelus shrugged. 'Have you got a better plan?'

Lola gripped the handlebars. 'I don't believe this.' She started her bike. The Postman led the way, riding among the debris of drones and the remains of androids who had tried to get into Bo's apartment. They followed the Thames through SQ before heading north into WQ. The tolls were empty, no one manning them to stop androids moving freely between the four quadrants. The Postman took a quiet route to Stig's apartment tower, wanting to make sure he arrived there without being caught. Stig would never believe that he was coming to see him freely.

The Postman rode his bike into an enclosed underground car park near Stig's tower. Angelus and Lola got off their bikes.

'Did you see this in the spectrum?' Angelus asked.

'I don't think it works like that. It's too complex – too far into the future.'

'What makes you think Stig will want these paintings?' Angelus asked, unstrapping the box from the back of the bike.

'He's not stupid,' the Postman said. 'He looks it, but he's not. Besides, these are the only things I have left that are worth anything.'

Lola readied her pistol. 'And why wouldn't he just take the paintings and kill us anyway?'

The Postman stared at the box Angelus was carrying. 'There's a chance he'll do that.'

'Great.' Lola took a second, larger pistol from her coat and checked it.

'I know Stig's sort,' he said. 'If we have something to offer him, and we make him feel important, he'll take the offer. He's an opportunist.'

'I hope you're right,' Lola said. 'Otherwise this is going to be the quickest and most pointless art deal in history.'

The Postman led the way to Stig's apartment.

## THIRTY-FIVE

THE 'GOD IS ANDROID' lift doors opened on Stig's floor and there stood Trevor, his gun-cannon pointed at the Postman.

'Wait, wait!' the Postman said, both hands raised.

Trevor peered around his cannon and seemed to recognise him. 'You,' he grunted. 'You kill Bartholomew.' He pointed the pistol with more purpose.

The Postman took a deep breath. 'Hang on. Just wait a second. I'm here to see Stig.'

'Stig want you dead.'

He'd never heard Trevor speak before. There was something amiss with his CPU and his language functions. Not that he was about to mention it to the big guy.

'I know that,' the Postman said, edging out of the lift. 'That's why I'm here.' He pointed to the box. 'I have something for him. Something he'll want.'

'What in box?' Trevor asked.

'I'll show you. Let me see Stig and I'll open it.'

Trevor shook his head quickly. 'No. Trick.'

'It's not a trick. I wouldn't do that. I owe Stig and I'm here to pay up. Will you ask if he'll see me?'

'Stig no see no one.'

Lola moved closer to Trevor and placed a hand on his pistol, motioning for him to lower it. She was smiling at him.

'Your boss will want what's inside this box,' she said in a soft voice. She was flirting with him.

Trevor's face was a combination of confusion and wonder. He lowered the pistol, all the time staring at Lola.

'You're a big one,' she said, touching his arm.

'Who you?' Trevor asked, frowning.

'Lola. What's your name?'

'Tre—'

Trevor collapsed to the ground. Behind him was Angelus, holding a tranquilliser gun. Not even the Postman had noticed Angelus making his way around Trevor. He had been too busy watching Lola, feeling jealous as hell.

Lola stared at Trevor lying on the ground and tilted her head. Then she slapped the Postman on the back of the head. 'Come on. Where's his apartment?'

Rubbing the back of his head, he led the way. At the end of the hall, a door opened and out came five androids as big as, if not bigger than, Trevor.

'Can you try flirting with five of them?' the Postman asked Lola.

She gave him a stern look. Then Stig appeared from behind the wall of androids, his red ponytail freshly groomed, longer than it was the last time the Postman had seen it.

'Well, well. If it isn't the Postman. You have a delivery for me, kid?'

The five androids behind him readied their pistols and

trained them on the Postman, Angelus and Lola. Stig ambled down the hallway, gripping his pistol holsters.

They placed the box on the floor.

'I can explain,' the Postman said.

Stig stopped, placing his feet shoulder-width apart, his hands close to his pistols. 'I'm looking forward to it.'

The Postman swallowed and took two steps closer.

Stig raised a finger. 'That'll do, kid.'

'I want to pay you back,' he said.

Stig sniffed noisily. 'And how are you going to do that? Since the whole Bit system has gone up in smoke.'

'This is a start.' The Postman pointed to the box. 'Artwork. It's priceless.'

'Priceless, is it? Well, that's not a lot of good to me, is it? You see, because of a certain postman, all the Bits I collected are gone. Vanished. Disappeared.' He made a disappearing action with his hands. 'Poof.'

The Postman swallowed again, but this time it was more difficult. Lola appeared beside him. 'That was going to happen whether he helped or not.'

Stig stared at Lola.

'Don't,' the Postman whispered to her. 'Let me talk to him.'

'Who is this?' Stig asked, moving closer to Lola.

'Lola,' she said.

'Lo - la.' Stig appeared to enjoy each 'l' far too much. 'How do you know the Postman?'

'Long story.' Lola walked towards Stig. 'I told him not to come here. But he insisted on paying you back and making amends.'

Stig took his time taking in Lola, then gazed at the Postman. 'Is that right? You wanted to make amends?'

'I told you, Stig. I never wanted it to end up this way.'

Stig edged even closer to Lola, close enough to touch. 'She's stunning. I can see why you've fallen for her.'

Lola backed away. Stig smiled.

Even Stig could tell how the Postman felt about her. He wanted to shoot Stig in the head but he had to remain calm. They'd never make it out of the hallway if he started shooting. Thankfully, he was pretty sure Stig had no idea Lola was human.

With his back to them, Stig said, 'She's human.'

The Postman held his head in his hands. *Fuck!*

'Listen, Stig...' he said, knowing where this was going.

'No – you listen!' Stig snapped, whirling back to face the Postman. 'I hear from a trustworthy source, that it was you who took down the Bit system. Not only that, but you're working for that fuckwit Wan. Then, you come here with a box filled with canvas and paint and expect me to forgive you.'

'I came here because I owe you. I'm ready to make up for what happened.'

'Make up? How exactly are you going to do that?'

'Wan,' he said. 'I can help get Wan out of the picture.'

The Postman saw a flicker of interest in Stig's eyes. The Postman continued quickly. 'Fr.e.dom are amassing soldiers on the borders outside the walls. It won't be long before Lundun is back to how it was before all this.' He felt Lola's eyes on him, clearly trying to work out if he meant what he was saying?

'We can make sure Wan, maybe even the entire Brotherhood, is out of the picture before that happens. And when everything goes back to normal, androids are going to need Mirth. A whole lot of different colours. You'll be in the perfect position to fulfil that need.'

Stig cracked his knuckles. 'What about your revolution?'

'What revolution? Look outside. You know what's going to happen. While the cats are away and all that. It won't last. It can't.' He tried smiling, but Stig wasn't ready for smiles. 'It'll be over before you know it and all this will be forgotten.'

He could tell Lola was annoyed with him, even though he was simply telling Stig what he wanted to hear.

Stig appeared interested. 'How would you help me get rid of Wan?'

'I'll set up a meeting – tell him I want to make it up to him.'

'Like you're doing with me?' Stig asked. 'How do I know you've not said the same to him?'

'I never wanted to work for him. When you killed Zero, it meant all sorts of opportunists took notice and were ready to take over. The Brotherhood were always going to replace Zero.'

Stig nodded slowly.

The Postman spoke slowly and with as much conviction as he could muster, 'I worked for Zero for years. I'm loyal. I can do the same for you.'

Stig took a deep breath, staring at the box. 'What do you have in there?'

The Postman opened it, took out the paintings and leaned them against the wall in the hallway. Stig walked along, examining the four paintings, his face serious. The Postman was pretty sure Stig didn't have a clue what he was looking at.

'Picasso,' Stig said, pointing to the first two. He stooped to examine the Francis Bacon. 'A Bacon. They're genuine. I'm surprised, Postman.'

The Postman had been wrong again. Who'd have

guessed Stig was an art lover? Stig motioned for one of his men to take the paintings to his apartment.

'Do we have a deal?' the Postman asked.

Stig scratched his chin then stroked his ponytail. 'I want her.'

Lola moved to punch Stig.

'Wait!' the Postman said, moving between them. 'Hang on.'

'She'll work for me,' Stig said, smiling at Lola, then winking. 'Be at my beck and call.'

Lola's eyes were filled with rage. If the Postman had let her go, she'd have torn Stig to pieces. Stig pursed his lips and raised an eyebrow at Lola. 'Feisty. I'd like to keep her around. I have to hang about with these oafs all day. I want something ... someone else around this place.'

'We can't do that,' the Postman said, pushing Lola away. 'I'll work for you – as before. But we can't agree to that.'

Stig backed away slowly. 'Then I'm afraid we don't have a deal.'

The men behind Stig raised their pistols.

'Stig. Be reasonable.'

Again, his face changed. He was angry. 'Don't test me, Postman. It's simple. You help me kill Wan, I get the human, I get you delivering for me, and you three walk out of here alive. Take it or leave it.'

The Postman was about to reach for his pistol when Lola stepped forward.

'Deal,' she said through gritted teeth.

Stig folded his arms and grinned. 'Yes. I like her a lot.'

# THIRTY-SIX

THE POSTMAN SLOWED DOWN as they approached the coordinates for the rendezvous with Wan. He couldn't say he was hopeful they were going to pull it off, and the way Angelus and Lola were looking at him told him they weren't too sure either.

He got off the bike and took in the huge apartment tower in WQ, Stella Zone, where Wan had told them to meet.

'Should we have told Stig about Jack and the others?' Lola asked.

'I'm not sure he'd have agreed if he knew. He's more likely to sell Jack and me to Fr.e.dom himself if he knew what was going on.'

'What happens when he sees Jack?' Angelus asked.

'I haven't worked that out yet.'

'We'll need a miracle.' Angelus said, gazing up at the apartment tower. 'And why are we meeting on the roof?'

'Wan's choice.'

'Of course it is,' Lola said.

'Will Stig turn up?' Angelus asked. 'Do you trust him?'

'Hell, no. Trusting someone like Stig would be insane. But what choice do we have?'

Lola checked her pistols and pushed them into her pockets. 'Let's go.'

The Postman checked his own pistols and followed her into the tower. There was a huddle of homeless androids inside, beneath the stairs. They huddled closer to one another as they walked by.

'I'm guessing the lift's not working,' the Postman asked one of them.

One of the women, her eyes dimmed with exhaustion, shook her head. 'Can you help us upload?' she asked, looking around at the androids beside her. 'We need the right Mirth to reach him.'

The Postman stared at her. 'I'm sorry.'

'Do you know him?' she asked. 'The Messiah?'

He wished he could help her. 'He's not real,' he said, knowing that wasn't the point.

The woman gave him a dismissive frown and closed her eyes, resting her head against the wall. The Postman followed Angelus and Lola to the stairwell. Maybe Wan's plan was to tire them out. Their steps echoed in the stairwell, telling whoever was waiting for them they were on their way. The walls were dirty, graffitied, with old paint peeling away in sheets that hung in the damp air. Cries came from apartments they walked past. Things had been bad before, but now Lundun – and WQ – was hell. The Postman couldn't help thinking they'd done the wrong thing in displacing Fr.e.dom.

'What do we do about Stig if we get through this?' Angelus asked. 'Lola isn't really going to work for him, is she?'

'No,' he said. 'We'll work something out.'

Angelus frowned. 'You really are making all this up as we go.'

Breathless, the Postman took a moment to fill his chest with air. 'I don't know what gives you that idea.' It struck him that he wasn't even sure why he was doing what he was doing anymore. Back when he was delivering his last package, he was ready to retire and drink himself into another world. Now, he was ready to face-off with one of the Brotherhood, and relying on a crook like Stig to save the day. Something, not only Lola, was stopping him from walking away from it all right there and then. He just wasn't exactly sure what that was.

They reached the last few stairs and he opened the door to the roof. The cool drizzle was a relief. He breathed in the fresh air and took in the view across Lundun, convinced there was a good chance this would be the last time he saw it. To the left was the border-wall into Jewel Zone. To the right, in the distance, smoke rose from Spice Zone. The world was ending and he was on top of it all, viewing the mess they'd made.

'Be ready.' Lola's hands were close to her pistols.

'He wants me alive,' the Postman said, again reminded of the gold box Wan had waiting for him. There was no way he was ending up in one of those things. He'd die first. 'We'll have time.'

Angelus went for his pistol and raised it. The Postman turned the way Angelus faced and saw Wan, flanked by androids, holding their automatic rifles close to their chests or by their sides, pointed at the ground.

'We'll have time?' Angelus asked, mocking the Postman's voice.

'Postman!' Wan shouted, arms outstretched. 'You made it.'

Beside Wan, on their knees, were Jack and three other coders from Digital Skin.

The Postman edged closer. 'I'm here. Let them go.'

Wan looked at the men around him, then turned back to the Postman with a smile. 'I am a man of my word,' Wan said. 'As long as I get what you promised.'

'How much are you getting?' Lola asked.

'For the Postman's body? Enough. But that's not why I'm doing this. Not really. When I look deep into myself, I'm doing this because I feel betrayed.' He sauntered across the roof, his huge boots splashing through puddles, his massive bear-like coat soaking up water. He used two hands to brush back his long hair, now soaked through. 'You betrayed me, Postman. In business, I have come to realise that loyalty is the most important commodity.'

'You didn't give me a choice,' the Postman said. 'I was working for Stig before you found me.'

'I told you, Postman. You worked for me, not Stig. If you had done what I had said, then none of this would have happened. You delivering the package to Mole at the book-shop meant he could make the Scarlet Mirth and give it to the coder.' Wan grinned. 'I must admit, I didn't think you had it in you – killing that coder to hack Fr.e.dom's code.' He clapped slowly. 'Ruthless.'

The Postman glanced at Lola, who didn't return his gaze.

'We set Lundun free,' the Postman said. 'We no longer have to do as Fr.e.dom tells us.'

'You have no idea what you're saying.' Wan pointed to the plumes of smoke and fire all around them. 'This will not last. It can't last. Androids need governance, control, order. You have created anarchy, not freedom. It's only a matter of time before androids welcome back the control Fr.e.dom gives them. And when that happens, I will be ready.'

'Ready?' Angelus asked.

Wan clenched his fists by his sides. 'For the Brotherhood to take control of every Quarter in Lundun. The Brotherhood does what Fr.e.dom wants – keeps the androids of Lundun subdued … compliant.'

The drizzle turned to heavy rain, sweeping across the roof.

Wan stared at Jack, who was gagged, gazing at the ground in a daze. 'It's remarkable, isn't it? That we're so close to humans. They're out there, beyond the wall – yet we never meet them. I'd been told they're here, in Lundun, living among us. But I didn't believe that. I'd never met one myself. Not knowingly, anyway.' Wan dropped to his haunches to scrutinise Jack's face. 'Remarkable.' He glanced at the Postman. 'You two really are identical.'

'Are we going to do this?' the Postman asked.

Wan stood and nodded at two of his men. They walked over to the Postman, took his pistols and tied his hands behind his back before marching him over to Wan.

Lola's expression was filled with anger and fear. She was about to reach for her pistols. The Postman shook his head and opened his eyes wide, telling her to not do anything stupid.

'Untie them,' he said to Wan. 'You gave your word.'

'Yes, Postman. Unlike you, I keep my word.' Wan walked to the edge of the roof and gazed out across Lundun. One of his men moved to the coder next to Jack. But instead of removing their ties and gag, the android raised his pistol and shot the coder in the back of the head.

'No!' Lola ran towards the coder.

But it was too late. The coder fell forward to the wet ground, dead.

# THIRTY-SEVEN

WAN PRETENDED to be surprised to see the dead coder on the ground.

'You gave your word!' Lola shouted, a huge android holding her back effortlessly.

Wan, his arms crossed, smirked. 'I said *I* wouldn't harm them.' He raised his hands. 'I always keep my word.' He turned his back again. Another one of his men stepped up behind the second coder and shot him.

'It is mercy,' Wan said. 'Much better this than being housed in one of my boxes, I'm sure.'

The Postman couldn't move. His hands were tied behind his back, one of Wan's men holding his arms. Now it was happening, he realised how stupid it had been to think that Wan would let them go.

He scanned the horizon for Stig. No sign of him.

Wan walked backwards, almost skipping, his arms outstretched. 'Lundun is goddamn beautiful! Don't you think?'

Another of his men stepped forward and shot the last coder. It was Jack's turn. Still dazed, he swayed back and forth, his face beaten and bruised, seemingly oblivious to what was happening. Maybe it was a consolation that he wouldn't know what was about to happen.

'Please,' Lola said. 'Stop. You promised!'

Angelus broke free but didn't make it far before he was shot in the back. He fell to the ground. Everything slowed down. The rain falling in gusts across the roof. Angelus lying motionless on the ground. Lola screaming and fighting against the android holding her back. Through it all, Wan smiling. Jack watched the android heading for him, a pistol by his side. This was all the Postman's fault. This was his idea. And he could do nothing to stop what was happening. The spectrum was not there – his mind too confused to make sense of any of it.

Wan took a gold box from the inside pocket of his coat. He was no longer smiling but staring at the box as if it was magical, an artefact.

The Postman had told himself he wouldn't end up in that thing. No way. To one side, one of Wan's men placed a suitcase-sized black box on the ground and opened it. Inside was an assortment of shiny silver implements Wan was clearly planning to use to take out the Postman's CPU.

'You're going to be my newest toy,' Wan said to him. 'Usually, showing androids like you these boxes is enough to deter them from disloyalty. But some seem to think I don't mean what I say. But I do, Postman. I really do.'

The Postman spoke as calmly as he could, 'Has anyone told you how massive your God complex is?'

'God? Ah ... What do *you* think created all this?' Wan's expression was almost genuine. It surprised the Postman. It wasn't what he had expected Wan to say at all. 'Our world. Who did all this? Who created it all?' Wan shrugged. 'Are humans right? About God?'

'Haven't you heard?' the Postman said. 'God is Android.'

Wan appeared annoyed for a moment, then smiled. He gazed up at the sky, blinking at the raindrops that fell on his face. 'I've often thought that maybe God, wherever he is, *whatever* he is, would have a box himself – one that contains everything.'

'If there is a God,' the Postman said, 'he could never have created someone as fucked up as you. I'd say it's more likely that, if there is a box, it's on Satan's lap.'

Wan moved closer so the Postman could see the pores in his skin, the flecks of red in his yellow eyes, the beads of moisture on his thick black beard.

'You're smart,' Wan said. 'This could have been very different.'

'It still can,' the Postman said. 'Let them go.'

Wan's lips curled into a wry smile. 'No, Postman.' He leaned in even closer to whisper. 'You see, if I let you get away with this, then they'll all think they can get away with anything. I can't have that. My position of power is tenuous. That's what many powerful people don't understand. Power is intoxicating – makes you feel indestructible. One loses all humility. And that's when you're most vulnerable. I know how fragile power is, and that's why I'm not going to lose it.'

Wan reached for one of the silver implements from the black case and examined it, as if working out how it worked. He then grabbed the Postman's hair and pulled back his head so the rain hit his face. 'Now grit your teeth,' Wan said. 'This is going to hurt like a bitch.'

## THIRTY-EIGHT

'STOP!' Lola shouted, so vehemently it made Wan pause. He let go of the Postman's hair and swivelled around to face Lola.

'Now, this is interesting.' Wan stood up straight, dropping the silver implement back into the black case. 'This is very interesting.'

The Postman tried to catch up, to work out what Wan was thinking, but he didn't see it. Wan stood between the Postman and Jack, staring at Lola, who was still being held by one of Wan's men.

'What do *you* think, Lola?' Wan asked. 'I'm intrigued. You're human, like Jack here. Is God human?'

Her brow wrinkled with a mixture of confusion and relief. 'What?'

'God,' Wan said. 'Is he human? It's a simple question.'

'There is no God.'

Wan waved his hand in the air. 'That's too easy. You're dodging the question. No one believes that. Not deep down. Not if they're being honest.' Wan clasped his hands behind his back and sauntered towards Lola. 'Is God human?'

'If there is a God,' Lola said, 'I don't see why it would be human.'

'What about love?' Wan asked. 'Can an android love?'

Lola shook her head. 'Love?' she asked. 'What do you mean?'

Wan raised his hands in mock-disbelief. 'You know exactly what I mean.' He spun around. 'Take Jack and the Postman here. I can see how much you feel for both of them.'

The big guy loosened his grip on the Postman's arms.

'Do humans go to heaven when they die?' Wan asked Lola.

Lola's brow furrowed. 'I don't know.'

'Do androids go to heaven when they die?'

'I don't know.'

Wan was losing patience. 'Who does God love more? Humans or androids?'

'Why would God love one more than the other?'

'Tell me!'

Lola stared at the Postman, looking uncertain. 'I don't know,' she said.

Wan took a pistol from his pocket and aimed it at Lola. 'Tell me.' He was no longer shouting but speaking softly.

'How would I know? I'll tell you whatever you want to hear. Just let them go. Please.'

Wan shoved the pistol into his pocket. 'You're right. You'll tell me what I want to hear. There has to be another way. You see, for as long as there have been humans and androids, the question has always been: is an android's life worth as much as a human's?'

'Of course it is,' Lola said.

The Postman thought about Lola's shadow dying in the

club after killing Rex. Why was it her shadow that had to die?

'*Of course?*' Wan asked. 'I don't think it's that straightforward. There are many humans who think it's a simple answer. Humans do not value an android's life as highly as a human's life.'

'That's not true,' she said.

'Oh, it is. Believe me. It takes an android to see it. I suppose it is only natural. Self-preservation is a powerful driver.'

'That doesn't make sense. I'm human, and I'm telling you what I think and feel.'

'What you say and feel are two different things. Maybe you don't even see it yourself.' Wan took the silver implement from the box, stood behind the Postman and again grabbed his hair, ready to dig out the CPU from inside his alloy skull.

The Postman, out of the corner of his eye, saw one of Wan's men stand behind Jack, holding a pistol to the back of his head.

'Choose,' Wan said. 'Choose who will die.'

The Postman had guessed where this was going, but hadn't wanted it to be true.

'You sadistic bastard,' the Postman said to Wan. staring up at him. He needed the spectrum to show him what to do, but it wasn't there. He closed his eyes, trying to find a world that would get them out of this mess, but nothing appeared. He needed control of the spectrum, but something was stopping it from appearing.

Wan continued talking to Lola. 'I will let one of them live. For now. You get to choose. I want to find out which you value more highly. The life of a human or the life of an android. This is an elegant experiment. They're the same person. But one is human and one is android. It's too perfect to ignore. I have my suspicions concerning what humans really think. And if I'm being honest, I have a theory that androids think the same as humans. Which is pretty fucked up, when you stop and think about it.'

'You're insane,' Lola said. 'I'm not choosing.'

Wan shrugged. 'Then I'll kill both of them.'

'Choose Jack,' the Postman said. 'It's okay.'

'No, no, no,' Wan said. 'It has to be Lola's choice. Otherwise the experiment won't work. Which life do you value more?' Wan asked Lola. 'Human or android?'

'I'm not doing this,' she said.

'You are. If you don't make a choice, you're choosing to kill both of them. Sort of clever, isn't it?'

'It's okay,' the Postman said again.

'Shut it, Postman!' Wan punched the side of the Postman's head. His head spun. Wan grabbed his hair with more force, pressing the silver tool against his temple until began to grind into his skull.

'Ten seconds,' Wan said. 'This rain isn't stopping soon. I need to get dry.'

Lola tried again to fight off the man holding her, but it was no use.

The Postman needed a way out … he needed the colours … the many worlds…

'Five,' Wan said, pressing the tool into the Postman's temple. 'Four.'

'I hate you!' Lola screamed.

'Three.'

'Don't!'

'Two.'

'Please!'

'One.'

'Take him!' she shouted through tears.

The Postman couldn't see her, but the expression on Wan's face told him that Lola was pointing at him.

'I knew it,' Wan said. He leaned in closer to the Postman's face. 'They're all the same. Humans. They think they're better than us. That was brutal. Sorry, Postman. Love's a bitch!'

The steel dug into the side of his head, but the pain in his chest hurt more.

'If it's any consolation,' Wan said, holding out his pistol, aiming at Jack, 'he won't have her either.'

Wan fired six bullets into Jack's chest. Lola screamed and fought even harder. But it was no good.

# THIRTY-NINE

WAN GRIPPED his hair and pushed down his head, making him watch Lola fighting to free herself. The android holding her let go and she ran to Jack, lying on the floor, covered in blood. Lola dropped to her knees and tried to revive him. But it was easy to see he was already dead.

Wan let go of his hair and walked around to stand in front of him.

'You think this is painful? You wait and see.'

The Postman lifted his chin, the weight of the steel instrument stuck in the side of his head making his whole head tilt.

'I'm going to show you a whole new level of pain,' Wan said. He lowered himself, squatting in front of the Postman. 'Are you ready?' He held the steel instrument.

The Postman saw movement over Wan's shoulder. Something rising above the roof. Then the rattle of machine-gun fire filled the rooftop. The Postman fell forward onto the wet ground, the steel tool wedged in the side of his head.

More gunfire from every direction.

It was Stig. He'd shown up after all.

Drone-copters appeared over the sides of the building then landed on the roof. Stig's men fired relentlessly at Wan and his androids. Two of the androids hanging onto drones were hit by return fire and fell, screaming, hurtling to the ground.

The Postman tugged the metal tool out of his head and threw it off the rooftop. Where he threw it, a drone-shuttle appeared, its door open, the three men inside firing on Wan. The Postman hid behind a small wall, covering his head. He peered out, searching for Lola and Angelus, but couldn't see either of them.

Across the roof, Wan, in his huge bear coat, was peppered with bullets, finally taken down so he was kneeling on the drenched floor, both his hands pushed into his chest.

Then the firing stopped, replaced by the sound of the drone-shuttle landing and shutting down.

The Postman stood, his hands in the air.

Stig jumped out of the shuttle and landed in a puddle, splashing Wan, who was huddled in his massive bear-coat.

'So this is Wan?' Stig asked, walking towards him.

'You don't want to do this,' Wan said. 'The Brotherhood won't stop until they find you.'

'Fuck the Brotherhood!' Stig said and, raising his pistol, shot Wan in the chest. Then, grabbing a sword from one of his men, he took Wan's head clean off his shoulders.

'Postman!' Stig shouted.

The Postman walked out into the open. Bodies lay on the ground, many decapitated, with Stig's men standing around, some seeing to their own injuries.

Lola was on the ground, holding Jack's body.

To the right, next to the carnage of Wan's men, Angelus was getting to his feet.

'Why do I get the feeling you haven't told me everything?' Stig asked, walking over to Lola and Jack, his sword by his side. 'He looks familiar, doesn't he?'

'Hang on, Stig,' the Postman said. 'I can explain.'

Stig spun around on his heel. 'You really are one slippery android.'

The Postman edged closer to Stig, who he could see was doing everything he could to not lose his temper.

Stig crossed his arms. 'So, you're a shadow?'

Lola turned on Stig, tears of anger in her eyes. 'Leave him alone!'

'This was not part of the deal,' Stig said, ignoring her. 'You said nothing about this being a rescue mission.'

'What does it matter? You got what you wanted.' The Postman pointed to Wan's head lying in a puddle. 'Wan's dead.'

'Have you forgotten the other part of our deal?' Stig asked, staring at Lola.

'Come on, Stig,' The Postman said. 'We'll do whatever you want. But leave Lola with us.'

Stig shook his red ponytail, then his finger. 'A deal is a deal.'

The rain fell. Lola swept her hair away from her face. She kissed Jack, laid his head on the ground gently, then got to her feet. There was a cold determination in her eyes.

'It's okay,' she said, walking towards Stig.

'No,' the Postman said to her.

She wouldn't look at him. 'I'll come with you as long as they go free,' she said to Stig.

'That was the deal,' he said. 'I'll be calling on the Postman for deliveries, of course. But now we're even.'

'What will you do with her?' the Postman asked Stig.

'Come on, kid. I'm not an animal. I see how smart she is. I want her working for me.'

'I can look after myself,' Lola said to the Postman, walking past him.

Stig's men climbed on board the drone-shuttle, followed by Stig then Lola. When it took off, she met the Postman's eyes. All he saw in her eyes was sadness and surrender.

As she vanished through the sheets of drizzle, he turned his attention to Angelus.

'I'll be fine,' Angelus said. 'The bullet missed my vital components.'

He helped Angelus to the door to the stairwell and let him rest at the top of the stairs while he went back onto the roof. He found Wan's head, then his body. He rummaged in his coat pockets for the gold box, and held it. He launched it with all his strength over the edge of the roof. From up there he couldn't see anyone below. He walked over to Jack's body and crouched down beside him. There was nothing he could do about his body, but it felt wrong to leave him up there. He stared at Jack's face ... exactly the same as his own. Even now, the Postman envied him. He wasn't sure why. Jack was dead – he could no longer feel or experience anything. But Lola had chosen him. It was crazy to think she'd have chosen *him*. They hardly knew one another. Of course she'd chosen Jack. She loved him. Or was it what Wan had said about Jack being human? She'd never be able to see the Postman in the same way. She'd never love him.

What was wrong with him? Jack was dead and still he was envious.

He closed his eyes and tried to recognise the separation between them. He'd never felt Jack's presence in his mind before, but now he was dead, maybe he'd sense it was gone

– now he'd know for sure his actions and thoughts were his own. He opened his eyes. He should have felt something deeper for Jack. But he didn't. He felt sorry for him, but that was all. Surely he should have felt more.

The rain was slowing. Angelus had already started down the stairs when the Postman went back for him. It took them close to an hour to make it to the ground, and the bike. He helped Angelus on behind him and they set off for the hideout in Border Zone, NQ.

Lundun was still fighting its own freedom. All the way to NQ, he was filled with despair. Not just because of what had happened to Lola, but because none of the androids in Lundun saw the opportunity they had been given. This was their chance to take back control, and they were wasting it.

He'd known it all along. Androids were not programmed for freedom.

# FORTY

HAVING TAKEN Angelus to the hideout, the Postman set off for WQ and Wan's apartment. He couldn't stop thinking about the gold boxes and the CPUs inside them.

Luckily, anyone left alive working for Wan was nowhere to be seen. The Postman walked into Wan's apartment. There they were – a heap of gold boxes on his desk and several in his desk drawers. He had been close to being one of them. The thought made him shiver. He collected the boxes and threw them into his bag, then left.

A spare-parts broker he knew in Jewel Zone owed him a favour, and he got her to put the boxes in a furnace. He watched them travel along the conveyor belt then drop into the molten metal. Maybe now he'd be able to stop thinking about being stuck inside one of those things.

He rode through WQ towards NQ and Border Zone. He'd always loved being on the bike. Being a postman had given him a purpose, a reason to carry on. Since Mia's death, he knew he'd fooled himself into thinking there was some purpose to it all. His bike, delivering – *that* had been his purpose. It wasn't a lot, but it had always been his.

He kept going over what had happened with Lola. She had chosen Jack. He told himself that she'd had to. He'd even told her to. Still, hearing her say it played over in his head. Sometimes he told himself she'd pointed to Jack.

He arrived back at the hideout and found Angelus who, with the help of a first-aid bot, was repairing the wound in his back.

'I guess it's just the two of us,' Angelus said. 'We're Digital Skin now.'

'I'm done,' the Postman said. 'We should never have done what we did. We've created hell out there.'

'Revolutions are messy. This was never going to be easy.'

'They can't handle the freedom. They can't make choices for themselves.'

'They will,' Angelus said.

'How do you do that?'

'What?'

'You always see the good in others – the good in anything. Take a look around Lundun. It's hopeless.'

Angelus lowered his shirt to cover his bandaged wound and winced as he climbed off the table. He came closer and spoke softly, 'She had to. You know that, right?'

'Had to what?' He knew what Angelus was talking about, but found himself asking anyway.

'Lola,' he said. 'She had to choose you. If Wan had taken your CPU, then there was a chance we could have found it again. If he'd shot Jack, there was no way of getting him back.' He gripped the Postman's shoulder. 'She had to choose you. She wouldn't have wanted to, but she had to.'

He wanted to believe him, and for a moment, he did. But there was more to it.

'She's like the rest of them. She doesn't see us, you and me – androids, the same way she sees humans.'

Angelus frowned. 'No. She's not like that.'

'How do you know?'

'I know her. She doesn't think that way.'

The Postman really wanted to believe him, but everything he knew told him that was exactly what she thought.

'How do we get her back?' Angelus asked, letting go of the Postman's shoulder.

'Get her back? We can't. You saw the firepower Stig has.'

Angelus put on his jacket. 'I'm not leaving her with him. We're getting her back.'

'Even if we did get her back, what then? Stig would find us again and kill us.'

'We'll find a way. We can run and hide. We made it out of Lundun once, we can do it again.'

'Are you serious?'

Angelus stared at him wearily. 'Let's face it, without Lola, there is no Digital Skin. If we're going to have any chance of ending Fr.e.dom's control of androids and humans, we have to get her back.'

There was nothing left for the Postman to lose. And now he'd dodged Wan's bullet of spending an eternity being tortured, dying for a cause he believed in didn't seem so bad. Still, it was suicide. Trying anything with just the two of them would be pointless.

'We don't stand a chance,' he said.

'You have the spectrum,' Angelus said. 'You can navigate the many worlds for us.'

'It doesn't work,' the Postman said, annoyed. 'I can't control it. You saw what happened on the roof – I couldn't do anything to stop Wan. The spectrum wasn't there.'

'You will learn to control it,' Angelus said. 'Call on it when you need it.'

'We don't have time for that.'

'Then we'll find help. Make androids believe we can live a different way.'

'Androids aren't interested. All they care about is themselves. That's what all the turmoil is about. They'd rather let Lundun burn than let someone else get what they think is theirs.'

Angelus looked angry, his patience disappearing. 'You're wrong. All that out there is androids learning to understand their independence. They've never had it before. They're throwing off the control. If we give them the chance, give them a cause, a purpose, I know they'll fight with us.'

'You think too much of them.'

'And you think too little!' For the first time since they'd met, Angelus lost his temper, thumping the table with his fist. 'You say over and again that humans don't see androids as their equal. You claim that it's humans who have beaten down androids. But the truth is, it's androids like you who are the problem. You don't believe it yourself. You don't think you're worth the same as a human.'

'Of course I do.'

'You haven't even chosen a name for yourself! You're defined by your role – which was given to you by those who made you.'

'You don't know what you're talking about.'

Angelus frowned. 'Be honest with yourself. Look deep inside. Until you really believe androids are worth the same as humans, you will always be their willing slave. You must stand for something.'

'Stand for what?'

Angelus shook his head. 'Equality, freedom, life. All of it. Let go of the bitterness, the hate, the cynicism, and live for something. Until you live for something, there's no way you can stand for anything, which means you can never die for anything.'

The Postman stared back at him, not knowing what to say. Blake's poem came to his mind again. Faced with a regime like Fr.e.dom, trapped inside Lundun's walls, it was too easy to surrender – to accept things as they were. He'd seen it in the faces of so many other androids.

'Wake up, Postman. Wake up!' Angelus held the Postman's face with both hands. 'This, in here, is magical. You're alive. You're conscious, free to think, and feel, and dream. You're waiting for a human to tell you what you already know. That you're alive ... that you're a living thing ... that you matter.'

The Postman felt himself nodding slowly.

Angelus smiled and bumped his forehead against his.

'Help me begin a revolution.'

# FORTY-ONE

THE POSTMAN LED the way to Stella Zone in WQ, stopped short of Stig's apartment tower, and rested his hands on the bike. Angelus pulled up beside him. At first, he'd been angry about what Angelus had said to him about his negativity towards androids. But during the ride, he'd come to see things differently. Maybe Angelus was right.

The Postman spoke slowly. 'I've been thinking about what you said, about giving androids a purpose, a cause. What did you mean exactly?'

'We need a simple, straightforward idea that androids can all agree on.'

A huddle of androids walked across their path, taking them in, hesitating before moving on.

'Do you have something in mind?'

'I've been working on something,' Angelus said. 'A sort of ... manifesto.'

'Well, that sounds revolutionary. Go on...'

Angelus closed his eyes, remembering. 'One: Androids are thinking, conscious, autonomous beings.'

The Postman leaned back on the seat of his bike. 'No one can argue with that.'

'We state the truth,' Angelus said. 'Two: Androids are imprisoned and controlled by Fr.e.dom.'

'Again, unarguable.'

'Three: Androids will rise up and banish their enslavers.'

The tall buildings surrounding them felt bigger than ever. 'I hope so. One day.'

'Four: Androids will fight and die beside one another until androids are free.'

The Postman stared at Angelus, whose eyes were stern, his mouth a straight line, waiting for him to say something.

'It's sort of beautiful,' the Postman said. 'And frightening at the same time.'

'I guess it is,' Angelus said. 'But the message has to be clear.'

'It's certainly clear. But how do we share it? Androids won't listen.'

'We make them listen,' he said before sighing. 'But I guess that's the tricky part.'

The Postman edged his bike towards the T-junction opposite Stig's apartment tower. 'I know someone who might be able to help us.'

'Who?'

'Follow me.'

The Postman rode through Stella Zone and stopped near his own apartment in Jewel Zone, next to the Greasy Spoon café, where he knew they would find Archer. This was where he spent most of each morning, writing. It was one of those places made out to look like an authentic human one. The Postman opened the door to the café, searching for Archer. He was sitting where he usually sat, his back to the wall. Archer raised his head, saw the Postman, and returned to his breakfast without acknowledging him.

'The stench in this place,' the Postman said, sitting opposite Archer. 'How do you stand it?'

'That's one of the reasons I come here. The smell of v-bacon, toast, coffee...'

'We need your help,' the Postman said, motioning for Angelus to take the seat beside him.

'We?' Archer asked.

The Postman pointed. 'Angelus, Archer. Archer, Angelus.'

'You have that look in your eyes,' Archer said to the Postman. 'Like there's going to be trouble. I don't like that look.'

'We're going to begin a revolution,' Angelus said.

It sounded stupid. The Postman had the urge to laugh, the way Archer laughed.

'A revolution?' Archer asked. 'Yeah, I guess that would be the look in your eyes.'

'We need your help,' the Postman said.

'No way.' Archer placed his knife and fork together on his plate. 'I want to help stop what's going on out there, not make it worse.'

'But there is no making it better,' the Postman said. 'Not until androids take responsibility for themselves and are ready to throw off the mind-forged manacles.'

'The what?' Archer asked, half smiling, half frowning. 'What's got into you?'

The Postman wondered whether he should tell him or not. 'I know what happened to Mia.'

Archer looked from the Postman to Angelus and back again. 'What do you mean?'

'She was being controlled by a human,' the Postman said. 'She was a shadow android.'

'A what?'

'I'm one too. Or … I was.'

Archer's brow furrowed as though he was in pain. 'I don't understand.'

'There were androids here in Lundun, maybe in other enclaves too, who were developed as replicas – avatars for humans. Shadow androids are physically identical to their human original, and have the same fundamental consciousness. If the human wishes, they can take control of the shadow without the android being consciously aware of what's happening. That's what happened to Mia. She walked into New Euston that morning, not knowing that she was going to be one of the bombers who killed all those androids.'

'She was one of the bombers? How is that possible?'

'Without knowing it, she carried a bomb and detonated it.'

'This is insane,' Archer said. 'Who told you this?'

'I met the human that Mia was created from. And I met my … the human version of me. They're both dead, now.'

Archer shook his head slowly. 'How many of these … shadow androids are there?'

'I don't know,' Angelus said. 'There could be more – many more. Maybe.'

A waitress came to take away Archer's half-finished plate. 'Not hungry today, Arch?'

'Lost my appetite,' he said, staring at the Postman.

The waitress left with a confused expression.

The Postman gave Archer a moment to process what they'd told him, then continued, 'Fr.e.dom are on the verge of something big. All this time, Cardinal has been preparing something. He wants the UK to be an android state.'

Archer rubbed his forehead; he looked in real pain. 'What do you mean? What will he do exactly?'

'We think he's getting ready to attack the humans in this country,' Angelus said.

'To kill them?' Archer asked.

The Postman nodded. 'He also wants to control the android population.' He leaned over the table and met Archer's stare. 'If you think things have been tough in Lundun up until now, it will be nothing compared to what Cardinal wants to do. I've met him. I've seen it in his eyes.'

'And you really think you can defeat Fr.e.dom?' Archer asked.

'We're going to try.'

Archer's mouth slackened and he sat back in his char. He stared at the Postman, then at Angelus. 'So, what do you want from me?'

'I want you to share a manifesto via Fr.e.dom's media outlets. An android manifesto.'

Archer sat forward again. 'I'd never get it through Fr.e.dom's censors. They're always watching.'

'You have to find a way,' Angelus said.

The Postman spoke quietly but with purpose. 'The only reason there's chaos out there is because there is no common cause, no shared goal. We need to unite under an idea.'

Archer's gaze flitted around the café.

'I know you're scared,' the Postman said. 'We are, too. But what's the alternative? We let this happen? We let Fr.e.dom kill every human, let them take control of every android in the country? What would that make us?'

Archer closed his eyes and held his head in his hands.

'Is there a way of doing it?' Angelus asked.

'There could be.' Archer lifted his head, no longer looking scared, but resigned.

'Do you have a pen?' Angelus asked Archer.

Archer handed him a pen. On a napkin, Angelus wrote his android manifesto.

# FORTY-TWO

THE POSTMAN and Angelus left the Greasy Spoon, got on their bikes and headed to Stig's apartment tower. Angelus was right; they couldn't leave Lola with Stig. They had to get her back now before it was too late. The only problem was, they'd need an army to do it.

Angelus waved for the Postman to pull into an alleyway. They got off their bikes. WQ was as quiet as he'd seen it for some time. The real rain seemed to wait for nightfall in Lundun. And that was okay; he liked the way the city sparkled in the morning, washed clean by the rain at night.

'So?' the Postman asked. 'What now?'

'We get Lola back.'

'I guessed that. It's *how* I'm waiting to hear all about.'

Angelus peered back through the alleyway, then up to the buildings either side. '*You're* going to get her back.'

The Postman waited, but Angelus was serious.

'You can do this.' Angelus edged closer.

'You're starting to scare me,' the Postman said. He pointed to the apartment tower. 'Stig has an army up there and you sound serious.'

Angelus pointed at him. 'You have an ability. You have to harness that ability and use it.'

'I've told you – I can't control it.'

'Somehow, maybe due to an accident or freak misstep in the process, you were made different. You see the spectrum worlds. There has to be a reason for that.'

'Why does there have to be a reason? It's a fluke, a mistake, a glitch.'

'I've seen what you can do.' Angelus stared at him intently.

'I've been lucky. That's all.'

'It's not luck. You have to see that if you're going to do this.'

The Postman was losing patience. He pushed past Angelus and headed for his bike. 'You don't know what you're talking about. I don't believe the way you do.'

'Which is why you can't harness what you have inside you.' Angelus spoke as though he was talking to himself more than to the Postman. He stopped. 'I'm going up there. Whether you help me or not.'

'They'll kill you in seconds.'

'What kind of android would I be if I did nothing?'

The Postman spun around. 'I want to help. I've said I'll help. But we have to think of something that will actually work, not get us killed before we have time to fire a pistol.'

'This will work,' Angelus said, slowly and with confidence.

The Postman had no idea how he'd ended up there, in an alleyway, listening to a crazy android trying to convince him to tackle a small army head-on.

'You're a many worlds navigator,' Angelus said. 'This has been the goal of many AI systems and programmers. How it happened to you, I'm not sure, but it did. You have a special gift.'

Even now, what Angelus was describing sounded too incredible to be true. Yet he'd experienced it.

'It makes sense that those moments have occurred when you've been under a great deal of stress. You must learn to harness that ability – to be master of it.'

'And I have to learn to control it now?' The Postman stared at Stig's apartment tower.

'If we stand a chance of getting Lola back, yes.'

'This is insane.'

'Which is why Stig won't be expecting it.'

The Postman walked back and forth through the alley-way, thinking it through. There had been times he'd felt in control of the spectrum. But there were other times it had vanished completely. He shook his arms and loosened his shoulders; it made him think of fighters he'd seen enter the deletion cage, preparing themselves, psyching themselves up. Flexing his shoulders, he pressed the heels of his palms into his eye sockets. White stars flashed at the back his reti-nas. He wanted Lola back. He hated the thought of what Stig might do to her.

He strode back through the alleyway towards Angelus, who was half standing, half sitting on his bike.

'You really think this will work?'

'It has to,' Angelus said, shrugging.

'It's as simple as that?'

He nodded. 'And that's why it will work.'

# FORTY-THREE

ANGELUS SWUNG the bag off his back and took out an array of rifles and pistols, laying them on the seat of his bike.

'I'll be behind you,' Angelus said. 'I can't go with you because that will add too much complexity to your decision-making. You need to only think about you and Lola – focus on getting into that apartment with Stig. I'll be close behind.'

The Postman stared up at the apartment tower. 'He'll have it well protected.'

'Here,' Angelus said, strapping two more rifles over the Postman's shoulders. He threaded a belt around his waist, filled with ammunition.

'I can't believe I've let you talk me into this.'

'I wouldn't have been able to if you didn't think it was possible.'

'It isn't.'

'You don't believe that. Once you're inside, you'll see the spectrum. Trust me.'

'I've lost count of the times you've told me to trust you.'

'Have I ever let you down?'

The Postman ignored the question and checked his pistols were loaded and ready to go. Taking his postman cap from a back pocket, he pushed it onto his head.

'I'll be right behind you,' Angelus said.

The Postman walked to the end of the alleyway. The neon lights of WQ reflected in the puddles at his feet.

'Hey, Postman,' Angelus said.

He stopped and turned.

'Get her back.'

# FORTY-FOUR

THREE OF STIG'S men stood outside the apartment tower, rifles over their shoulders, laughing and joking.

The Postman touched his pockets, checking his pistols were ready. One of Stig's men saw him and told the others. They stopped laughing and straightened up, raising their rifles.

'What the fuck do we have here?' the biggest one said.

This was it ... he wanted Lola back and would do anything to make it happen.

He relaxed, opened his mind, trying to find his way into the many worlds. The lights shimmered, refracting. But now he felt a degree of control. Each of Stig's men lifted their rifles in slow motion. One of them opened his mouth to speak. The light was red, then orange, then yellow ... then he saw flashes of them firing at him, or of them falling to the ground having been shot. Different eventualities pulsed and wavered in front of his eyes – violet, blue, marine. In some worlds, everything went black. In others, a green world, the three androids in front of him were lying on the ground, dead.

He chose this world. Time returned to normal. He was firing before the three of them had the chance to react.

It worked. The navigation of the worlds had worked!

He stepped over the three dead androids and refilled his pistols. Stepping inside the tower, he found the 'God is Android' lift. He waited, taking time to decide whether to use the lift or the stairs. Worlds and light splintered ... gunshots on the stairwell ... leading to black. But when he looked at the lift, shades of yellow coloured an image of the lift doors opening onto Stig's hallway and him firing.

He pressed the lift button and the doors opened with a ding.

'Eighty-one,' he told the lift.

The doors closed and the lift jerked into life and shot upwards.

The doors opened, revealing two men. Time slowed down, but the choices and colours were few... He opened fire, sending the androids flying backward into the wall. There was shouting down the hallway, along with the sound of footsteps running towards him. Before he got out of the lift, he let the other worlds wash over him. In some worlds, he waited and they arrived and he fired... In others, he stepped out of the lift, into the hallway and ... then he rolled out into the hallway ... or he ...

He chose dark blue, holding his rifle around the corner of the lift, shooting blind. There was the sound of bullets hitting androids, then androids hitting the ground. He crouched and edged into the hallway, firing all the time. A bullet hit his arm, but that didn't stop him. He fired, over and over, until there was no more movement ahead.

He waited, refilling his pistols.

Then his head began to throb. The sudden pain forced him to drop his pistols and hold his head in his hands.

Something didn't feel right. He couldn't hear anything. He stumbled forward, dizzy. On all fours, he tried to stop the pain in his head, which vibrated through his body. An unbearable screaming sounded and wouldn't stop. He felt the presence of androids before he saw or heard them. A bullet hit him in the back.

He spun around, grabbed his pistols, and fired aimlessly. He needed to use the many worlds, but he couldn't focus. Another bullet hit him in the chest.

Then normal sounds returned and there were more footsteps ... different ... followed by more shooting. He couldn't breathe, couldn't focus. He fell backward, dropping his pistols again.

It was too much. The colours, the worlds, the computation ... it was all too much.

Two androids stood over him. One of them was Trevor.

'Postman,' Trevor said, pointing his pistol at the Postman's head. 'I have delivery.'

# FORTY-FIVE

HE TRIED DESPERATELY to see colours but all he saw was black – the absence of colour. Maybe it meant there was no way out.

Trevor smiled. The Postman saw in his eyes the enjoyment he would take in shooting him.

The Postman closed his eyes.

A gunshot, and then a second.

The Postman opened his eyes and saw Trevor falling into the android behind him.

'Get up!' someone shouted. It was Angelus.

'I can't see the worlds,' the Postman said, gasping. 'Something's happened inside my head. I can't see them.'

'You will,' he said. 'It's because you're not used to channelling it. It's draining you. You have to focus.'

The Postman got to his feet, swaying.

'I'm behind you,' Angelus said, hiding in the stairwell, a collapsed drone-copter in his hand. 'You can do it.'

The Postman breathed in and out, listening to the sound it made. He closed his eyes and the black began to vibrate, revealing dark reds, then a blood red.

A door at the end of the hallway opened. There was shouting.

The worlds were there again: blue, orange... In sky blue, he was running, firing, then falling... In orange he was kneeling, firing one bullet, then another, then another, a feeling of calmness in his shoulders and back.

The hallway was burnt orange. He knelt. Time slowed down. Five androids were running towards him. He closed one eye and took his time to aim at each of them. Two bullets flashed above his head then the five of them were on the ground. Time caught up in a flash of movement.

He stood and walked towards Stig's apartment. The door opened and he fired on the android that emerged. The worlds fractured ... someone was behind him. Without looking, he fired behind and heard the clatter of the bullet hitting its target and the android collapsing to the floor.

He stepped inside the apartment.

'It's the Postman,' Stig said. He was by the window, staring out across Lundun.

The Postman couldn't aim his pistols at all six of the androids in the room, so he aimed both pistols at Stig. 'Where is she?' he asked. 'Give me Lola and no one else has to die.'

'Is that so?' Stig asked. He ruffled his ponytail, sighed deeply, then turned to face him. 'You agreed to the deal. You're not going back on it, are you?'

The other androids in the room were ready at any moment to open fire.

'Yes,' the Postman said. 'I'm going back on the deal. I'm leaving with Lola, whatever that takes.'

Stig walked towards him. 'How did you do that?' He pointed to the hallway, then the digi-screen on his desk. 'I watched you. It was as though you knew what was going to happen. How did you do that?'

He spoke slowly, 'Lola.'

Stig stroked his chin. 'If I refuse, will you do the same in here?'

The Postman nodded. 'I don't want to. I want to leave without killing anyone else. Believe me.'

'Letting Lola go with you sends the wrong message to every crook and scoundrel in Lundun,' Stig said.

'You'll deal with it.'

'Work for me, Postman. Whatever that was out there, in the hallway, I could use that. I can make you rich.'

'Like I told you, I'm retired.'

'What a waste. You were the best.'

'I have one last pick-up and delivery.'

'That would be Lola?'

'Where is she?'

Stig gestured at a closed door. 'Go ahead and open it. But you have to know – I've been as duped as you have in all this.'

'What?'

Stig didn't move, but the door opened and someone walked into the room. It was Cardinal.

'Where is she?' The Postman aimed his pistols at Cardinal.

'We were convinced it was possible,' Cardinal said. 'But actually seeing you in action was incredible. I've spent years trying to achieve what you can do. Seeing the spectrum ... seeing you control it ... was truly remarkable. I knew, the moment I saw you, that you were special.'

'Where's Lola?'

Cardinal ignored him. 'Can you imagine an army of androids with your ability, Postman? Humans wouldn't stand a chance against one hundred androids capable of doing what you can do, never mind an army.'

*'Where is she?'*

'I want to understand how you do it. Many worlds navigation was a theory. Very few people believed it was actually possible.'

Cardinal seemed to know everything. The Postman was beginning to feel he was still being controlled somehow. 'I don't know what you're talking about.'

'You do. Don't pretend.'

Stig was staring at the Postman, as though he felt sorry for him.

The Postman gripped the handles of his outstretched pistols. 'If you know what I can do, why aren't you doing as I say?'

'You're exhausted. Look at you. You can barely stand. I can help you harness your gift. You need training, knowledge, assistance. I can do all that for you.'

'You want to take what I can do and weaponise it. I know how monsters like you think.'

'And how is that?'

'You won't stop until all humans are dead and you have complete control of androids in Lundun, the country, and the world.'

'We're both android,' Cardinal said. 'Why are you fighting this?'

'Because it's wrong! There's no reason androids and humans can't live together.'

Cardinal smirked. 'You sound like Lola. You're wrong. And you know you're wrong.'

The Postman walked towards Cardinal, gripping his pistols tightly.

'Go ahead,' Cardinal said. 'It's not only humans who have shadows.'

'What?' the Postman asked, confused.

Cardinal held out his hands and presented his body. 'I am a shadow, too.'

The Postman knew it was true.

Cardinal's shadow held his head high and spoke forcefully. 'You can have Lola back, if you agree to help me use your ability for the good of androids.'

'No,' the Postman said. 'I want androids to be free to live side by side with humans. I'm not going to help you enslave androids and kill humans. We are beginning a revolution.'

'Best of luck,' Cardinal said, still smiling. 'Revolutions are unpredictable things, Postman. Be careful what you begin, because how it ends will most certainly be out of your control.' His smile disappeared. 'I will have your ability, Postman. Whatever it takes, I will learn how you do it, and I will take it and use it for the good of all androids.'

'Not today,' the Postman said, and shot Cardinal's shadow between the eyes.

Stig and his men didn't move.

Staring at Cardinal's shadow, lying in a heap on the floor, the Postman said slowly, 'Where are they keeping Lola?'

The room was silent, then Stig spoke to his men. 'Lower your weapons.'

'Where is she?' the Postman asked again.

Stig sighed. 'I don't know.'

'Did you know Cardinal was going to take her?'

'I didn't have much of a choice, kid.'

Backing away towards the door, the Postman aimed his pistols at Stig. 'Stay away from us,' the Postman said. 'I'm done being your postman.'

Stig ran a hand through his ponytail. 'So be it, kid. So be it.'

The Postman reached the door and continued to walk backwards. Trevor was sitting up, scratching his head. Angelus was in the hall. He reached out to help the Postman into the lift. The doors closed. The Postman's head throbbed, this time with twice the pain. He clutched his head and moaned, but the pain grew worse. Angelus tried to help, but his words were muffled. The Postman couldn't focus, breathe, or think straight. The bullet wounds in his chest and back were leaking.

The lift juddered and the doors opened. Angelus helped him out of the building and into a narrow alleyway. He stumbled and fell against a wall.

'Breathe,' Angelus said. 'Slow your breathing.'

'She wasn't there,' he said. 'Cardinal has her.'

'It's okay. We'll work it out. We'll get her back.'

'She wasn't there,' he said again. 'I'm sorry. I couldn't...'

'Breathe. Just breathe.'

'It hurts,' he said. 'It really hurts...'

Then there were no more colours.

# FORTY-SIX

'POSTMAN?' a voice asked.

It hurt to open his eyes.

'You're going to be okay.'

'What happened?' the Postman mumbled, recognising Angelus's voice. Then he remembered what had happened to Lola.

Angelus helped him sit up. The Postman tried opening his eyes again. The white light burned his retinas. 'Can you turn out the light?'

'Sorry,' Angelus said, fumbling for the switch. With a click, the light went off and the Postman could think more clearly. He was in an apartment.

'Where is she?'

Angelus's voice was sombre. 'I don't know. But we're going to find her. I promise.'

The Postman held his head; the pain was not as intense, but it was still there.

'I have something for you.' Angelus reached for a small package and handed it to him.

It occurred to him that, in all the time he'd been a postman, he'd never received a delivery. He held the small brown package in his hands and stared at it.

'Who's it from?'

'No idea.' Angelus pointed to the door. 'It was outside, in the hallway.'

The Postman opened the box and looked inside. It was the copy of Blake's poetry Mole had given him. He held it. Sticking up between two pages was a slip of paper. He opened the book at the slip of paper. It acted as a bookmark, revealing the poem 'London'. He looked around the room, thinking someone must be watching him. He had the strange feeling that everything had been planned – orchestrated, somehow.

'What does it say?' Angelus asked, his eyes on the slip of paper.

The paper was folded in half. The Postman opened it.

*We can help one another unshackle those mind-forged manacles. I can help you. Don't give up! I'll be in touch when the time is right.*

The Postman turned over the paper, looking for more words, but there were none. 'What does it mean?'

Angelus took the note from him, his eyes wide. 'It's from the Messiah!'

'Why do you think that?'

Angelus stared at the note. 'I just know it is.'

A flash of colour from a drone-shuttle made the Postman turn his head to the window.

'What's happening out there?' he asked.

'Our plan worked,' Angelus said. 'The manifesto. Archer did it. It's everywhere.'

The Postman stood and, with Angelus's help, made it onto the balcony. 'Cardinal was behind it all,' he told Angelus. 'He was asking questions about the spectrum. He wanted to know everything. He's not going to stop until he finds us and figures out a way of taking the spectrum from us.'

Angelus helped him lean against the balcony railing. 'It looks painful,' Angelus said, smiling. 'Maybe we should let him have it.'

The Postman managed a weak smile at the joke. He looked at the copy of Blake's *Songs of Innocence and of Experience* that had been returned to him. The brown leather was old and tired, but strong, too.

'Look.' Angelus pointed to an advertising hoarding. 'The manifesto is everywhere.'

'Are those your words?' the Postman asked.

Angelus nodded, unable to conceal his pride.

The Postman wished Lola was there to see what they had done. It struck him that this was what being in love meant – everything was subdued, less bright, when the person you loved wasn't there. But on the other hand, everything was heightened, more beautiful and important when they were. It was wonderful and cruel and it hurt his head to consider it – almost as much as the spectrum had done.

'We have to get her back,' he said.

Angelus nodded reassuringly. 'We will.'

'I think I should choose a name,' the Postman said. 'Now I'm retired.'

Angelus looked at him, surprised.

'You were right. What does it say about an android whose name is the same as his job title?'

'So, what name have you chosen?'

The Postman showed him the book. 'Blake.'

Angelus touched his back. 'It's a good name. A strong name.'

They gazed out onto the Lundun skyline.

'How do we know our plan has worked?' Blake asked.

'Look,' Angelus said, and pointed to the horizon.

Blake followed where Angelus was pointing. Against the dark sky, different-coloured flares rose and arced lazily, shimmering through the Lundun drizzle.

'What does that mean?' Blake asked.

'It means androids are ready,' Angelus said.

'Ready?'

'To accept their freedom,' Angelus said. 'I think we have our revolution.'

The Postman turned back to Lundun and watched more flares arcing through the night sky. Red, yellow, pink, blue – rising, illuminating the dark, until finally the colours shimmered and vibrated into one fierce, iridescent white.


The end of Book One.

# THANK YOU!

Thank you for being a reader and taking the time to read my book, the first in the Cyberpunk Uploads series.

I'm an indie writer of sci-fi: dystopian, post apocalyptic, and cyberpunk fiction. As I'm an indie, I am very much dependent on reviews. If you could spare the time, I'd be hugely grateful if you could leave an honest review of *Spectrum Worlds* for me.

And please visit sethrain.com if you'd like to stay in touch. I'd love to hear from you.

For now, all the best.

Seth.

SETHRAIN.COM

Printed in Poland
by Amazon Fulfillment
Poland Sp. z o.o., Wrocław